THE GAME

by the same author

THE REWARD GAME
THE REVENGE GAME
FAIR GAME

THE GAME

Gerald Hammond

St. Martin's Press
New York

THE GAME. Copyright © 1982 by Gerald Hammond. All rights reserved. Printed in the United States of America. No part of this book may be used or reproduced in any manner whatsoever without written permission except in the case of brief quotations embodied in critical articles or reviews. For information, address St. Martin's Press, 175 Fifth Avenue, New York, N.Y. 10010.

Library of Congress Cataloging in Publication Data

Hammond, Gerald.
  The game.

  I. Title.
PR6058.A55456G3 1982 823'.914 82-16800
ISBN 0-312-31590-2

First published in Great Britain by Macmillan London Ltd.

10 9 8 7 6 5 4 3 2

THE GAME

One

Pressure for space, allied to certain tax advantages, had long since persuaded Keith Calder to remove the gunsmithing part of the business from the small shop in the square of Newton Lauder to his home a few miles outside the town. Thus it was from the open window of what had once been a master-bedroom in Briesland House that Keith was able to look across his garden towards the town and to enjoy the Scottish lowland scene under its July blanket of crops and wild flowers; but he was more pleased to look down and admire his infant daughter, kicking and crowing on her blanket in the shade of a huge beech tree, guarded by an elderly spaniel against the overtures of a younger dog

The room and its neighbour were given over entirely to fire-arms. Case after case displayed the antique guns which officially were stock-in-trade but of which Keith regarded the choicer pieces as being his personal collection. The desk and filing cabinets overflowed with catalogues and correspondence relating to original weapons, modern reproductions, kits and accessories. Beside the window was Keith's work-bench, the origin and pivot of the business.

On the bench was a superb North African jezail. Keith had finished patching in the missing scraps of ivory and mother-of-pearl in the inlaid stock and was touching up the engraving of the sliding flashpan-cover, when on one of his admiring glances he spotted the lanky form of his partner walking up the drive from a car parked outside the gates. By the time Wallace James arrived in the room the jezail was back in its case and Keith was concentrating on the innards of an English shotgun.

'If that's Mr C-carson's sixteen-bore,' Wallace said, 'the L-lancaster, he wants it back not later than yesterday.'

Keith refused to feel guilty. 'He can have it not sooner than tomorrow,' he said. 'Tell him he's knackered it.'

'Has he?'

'Nothing that a good clean-up and a new main-spring won't

fix, but tell him anyway. He'll be all the more grateful when he gets it back next week. Is Janet alone in the shop?'

Wallace nodded. 'Do you think Molly could g-go and give her a hand?'

When their two wives got together, conversation tended to take precedence over business. 'Better not,' Keith said. 'The customers wouldn't be able to get a word in edgeways. What brings you out here at this unlikely hour?'

Wallace fiddled aimlessly with a set of taps and dies and then slumped into a hard chair. His bony, intellectual face took on something of the look of a harassed horse. 'I'll t-tell you,' he said, and fell silent. He made a nervous gesture with his right hand, trying to run the missing fingers through his limp, brown hair.

Keith began to feel anxious. Wallace's slight natural stammer usually disappeared after the first few words unless he were very much disturbed. 'There's nothing wrong between you and Janet?' he asked.

Wallace shook his head. 'N-nothing like that.'

'The shop? Money?'

'I'm going to *t-tell* you, dammit,' Wallace said peevishly.

The door bumped softly open and Molly backed in with a tray holding coffee and three cups. 'I saw you arriving, Wal,' she said.

Wallace was usually at ease with his partner's wife – more so, sometimes, than with his own, whom he regarded as one of the miracles of nature. But on this occasion Molly's presence seemed to reduce him to a state of agonised incoherence and he only began to relax again when Molly, raising her eyebrows at Keith, finished her coffee and excused herself.

'All right,' Keith said. 'I get the message. There's something bloody far wrong, and it's confidential. You'd better spit it out.'

'Yes.' With a visible effort, Wallace pulled himself together. 'I'll have to think where to b-begin. You remember when we first met? I was between jobs and doing people's tax returns for pocket-money.'

'You still do,' Keith pointed out.

'It doesn't take up much time. N-not as much as you spend on your antiques.'

'That's part of the business!'

8

'Is it hell!' Wallace gestured around the cluttered room. 'You may kid the tax-man that this is all business stock, Keith, but you know and I know that the best pieces stick to your fingers. You jack the prices up above market value so that they won't get sold, and you make this side of the business wash its feet from the few that do fetch your asking-price and by spending a lot of time bodging up the damaged guns and flogging them again. Not that I'm c-complaining,' Wallace said hastily. 'Not as long as I make a living looking after the retail side. I just wanted to make you feel suitably guilty so that you'll help me out.'

'You don't have to do that,' Keith said. 'I'd help you out anyway.'

'N-not as a friend and a partner. I want to tap your expertise on behalf of somebody else. One of my clients dug this out of a chair-back.' Wallace took a matchbox out of his pocket and tipped out a small, lead ball. 'What could you tell me about it?'

Keith looked, and his eyebrows went up. 'It had been there a long time?'

Wallace hesitated and then decided in favour of frankness. 'The hole was new,' he admitted. 'And the chair isn't an antique.'

Keith smelled the ball and touched it with his tongue. 'You've washed it but there's no mistaking blood. Was that fresh too?'

'Do me a favour, just g-give me your opinion.'

'I'll do better than that, I'll give you my advice. Go to the police.'

Wallace made a face. 'It may c-come to that,' he said. 'I hope not, but it may. T-trust me, Keith, without asking any more questions. It's very, very important that we make sure it's necessary before we contact the police.'

'Blood and a bullet-hole, and you still aren't sure?'

'Somebody could have shot a . . . a cat,' Wallace said.

Keith shrugged. 'All right,' he said. 'For the moment, I don't know any different.' He got up and went to the window. Molly was with the baby on the lawn. He waved and then drew the curtains until only a thin slice of sunshine crossed the gloom, dancing with motes of dust. With this side-light to throw up the details, and with the aid of the powerful magnifier which was an important item in his tool-kit, he studied the ball minutely and then turned back to his bench. 'Right you are,' he said. 'Let there be light.'

Wallace pulled back the curtains, sat down again and watched patiently while Keith measured the ball, weighed it both in and out of a beaker of water and then repeated the process with a ball from his drawer.

'Got your calculator on you?' Keith asked. 'Do these sums for me.'

Wallace, who had started his working life as an accountant, carried a slimline calculator next to his heart. He pressed the buttons and read back a series of incomprehensible answers.

Keith perched up on the bench and studied his notes. 'Three hundred and seventy grains,' he said, 'which is near as dammit three-quarters of an ounce. It's slightly distorted, but the average diameter seems to have been point six of an inch. The specific gravity's the same as that of a modern, factory-made ball, so I can't tell you anything about the lead off-hand. Chemical analysis might be more helpful, whether it was mercury-hardened or whatever.'

'That would only home us in on a manufacturer,' Wallace suggested.

'No. This was home-made. Probably one of the cheaper Italian-made bullet-moulds – the two halves were very slightly out of register. The source of lead could be informative.'

'M-more to the point, what could it have been shot out of?'

'You don't want a lot, do you? See if this helps. There's very faint marks of rifling part of the way round one circumference. Probably six grooves, but there isn't enough to be sure. Not sharp enough to suggest that the ball was in contact with the rifling. I'd guess that the ball was enclosed in a cloth patch. Was the chair set on fire?'

'No.'

'Then the patch probably remained inside the ... the cat or whatever. Now, for the rifling marks to have been impressed through the patch, the ball plus patch must have been a pretty tight fit. There's a mark which suggests that it may have been rammed home with the blade of a screwdriver. That, in turn, suggests a pistol. After all, you don't use a screwdriver as a ramrod for something like a Tower musket, not unless you've got a screwdriver about four feet long. So you're looking for a pistol with a rifled barrel and no ramrod. Antique or reproduction. Possibly a Queen Anne screw-barrel and he'd lost the key, although the bore's a bit on the large side.'

'Definitely not a modern weapon?' Wallace asked gloomily.

'Why the hell should anyone load a modern weapon down the muzzle? Anyway, it's too big for anything smaller than an elephant-rifle.'

Wallace, who never swore, uttered three very rude words in startling conjunction. 'Can I borrow your barrel-gauge?' he asked.

'No you bloody well can't,' Keith said. 'It's stamped with my name, and I'm not having it found at the scene of a crime. I'm a respectable businessman, and I mean to stay that way in spite of you. I want my wild past forgotten. What's more,' he added, 'you're my partner now, and I want you to stay clean too.'

'I'd bring it straight back to you.'

'So you say. But suppose you were found on the scene? You know damn well you think there's been a serious crime. Go to the cops, Wallace. You don't have any choice.'

Wallace stared at him miserably. 'This is one of those impossible decisions to make,' he said. 'It's like being asked whether you'd rather be boiled or fried. I wish to God I knew what to do!'

Keith recognised the words as a cry for help. 'If you don't tell me what it's about,' he said, 'I can't give you any of that invaluable advice that you often ask for and never take.'

Wallace came to a reluctant decision. 'Will you come and look at something with me? And keep it totally and permanently confidential?'

'Where?'

'Less than an hour by car.'

'All right,' Keith said. 'But it's in confidence only as long as I don't get my head in a sling.'

Wallace brightened, just a little. 'That sounds safe enough,' he said. 'Let's go.'

When Keith told Molly that he was going with Wallace, she only nodded. Keith had been known to get into bad company.

Indeed, there were those who said that Keith himself was the worst of company. But he would be all right with Wallace.

They took Keith's car and Wallace directed him on to a by-road that ran, generally westward, from Newton Lauder towards the hills. Keith watched Wallace out of the corner of his eye. At first, Wallace seemed to have relaxed; then Keith saw signs of tension returning.

'Pull in and p-park,' Wallace said suddenly when Keith had been driving for half an hour.

They had just crested a hill. Keith found a layby to park. They sat for a moment looking over the valley ahead – woodland below, then fields and bare hills above. There was silence, broken only by the ticking as the exhaust contracted. Keith wound down his window, and tiny country noises crept into the car.

'I've been thinking,' Wallace said. 'Wondering how I c-could show you what you need to s-see and no more. But there's no way. So I'm going to spill the beans, in the strictest confidence, and if you ever utter a word without my express permission I swear I'll do something awful to you with a rusty razor-blade.' Wallace sounded as if he meant it.

'Cough it up,' Keith said. He prepared himself for a tale of some minor indiscretion which, to one of Wallace's retiring nature, would seem cataclysmic.

'You see that house there?' Wallace pointed to the slate roof of a large and rambling house, just visible among a froth of tree-tops. 'Do you know what that place is?'

'No,' Keith said.

'Then I'll have to go back a few years, to those days when I was in no sort of job and doing tax returns. Remember?'

Keith remembered. The loss of three fingers from his right hand had cut short Wallace's career in accountancy. When Keith met him, Wallace had been filling in time running an old barge.

'About eight or nine years ago,' Wallace went on, 'one of my first clients was a girl. I'd got some small shopkeeper out of trouble with the Inland Revenue and he'd been mentioning my name around, so she sought me out. And believe me, Keith, she was a stunner. She still is as a matter of fact. Genuine red-gold hair, a face that saw innocent and yet full of promise ... and if her

12

figure was unequalled, that was because God had decided that He'd never do better.'

'If this is a love story,' Keith said, 'You'd better confess it to Janet, not to me.'

Wallace gave a short bark of laughter. 'It might be a love story in your book but not in mine. She tried not to let on, but I soon guessed. She was a tart.'

'If you'd rather have my help than a thick ear,' Keith said, 'you'd better cut out that sort of crack. What was her problem?'

'The usual one – too much money which she hadn't told the tax-man about. She'd tucked away some savings in a deposit account, apparently on the advice of her bank manager. She was most indignant when he reported the interest to the tax centre as he's obliged to do. He hadn't mentioned that obligation to her. Snitching, she called it, when I explained. So, of course, the tax-men wanted to know where the money came from.'

'You told them?' Keith asked, fascinated.

'I decided not to. The legal position's a bit confused. There's a precedent for the proceeds of a crime being non-taxable, but prostitution isn't a crime in itself and anyway I wouldn't like to fight a case on it. Also, if you use the word "tart" in a tax return the inspector's beady eyes light up – not with lust but with an assessment of about a hundred grand a year. This girl had been making big money, but a pimp had had some of it off her and she'd spent a lot of the rest. If we'd made any sort of a truthful declaration, she'd have had the tax-inspector sitting at her bedside and counting the money for about the next ten years.

'So I spun a tale about her old job in hairdressing. It cost her some tax, which infuriated her, but she was off the hook – for that year.

'But the real trouble was that she'd been joined by a friend, another spectacular looker, and the two of them had been pouring money into their deposit accounts. I switched them to a building society, which is a different ball game, but the interest was already enough to curl the tax-man's hair, and come the following April the shit was going to hit the fan.

'So I took them to the races at Potobello with a wad of currency. I told them to turn the money over as often as they could. Losing a bit would be cheap at the price, what we wanted was a hell of a lot of cancelled winning tickets. Beginner's luck being what it is, they were about breaking even before the last race, backing a mixture of favourites and hunches. Then, in the last race, they had a flier on a horse called Ginger Tart and picked up a packet.

'We'd had a few drinks along the way, but when they realised that they could spend their winnings *and* make rude gestures at the tax-man, they started calling for champagne. But for that, I'd probably have kept my stupid trap shut. As it was, I couldn't remember half of what I'd said in the morning, and I couldn't have thought of it sober, but they had it all off by heart.

'Earlier, I'd been lecturing them on the dangers of sharing a flat, because that counts as keeping a brothel and *is* illegal. What they told me I'd said they should do, and even in the cold light of the following afternoon I couldn't find fault with it, was to buy an old house with a big garden, form themselves into a company, run a legitimate business in the house even if it lost money, put a couple of chalets in the garden and rent them from the company for the fun and games, pay themselves modest salaries, set up a pension fund and salt the rest away in short-term endowment policies.

'So that's what they did, in an old manse in Edinburgh. The other girl, Moira, had been masseuse and osteopath, so they ran the house as a health-and-beauty clinic and whored away in the chalets.

'They had neighbour troubles, of course, and other girls wanted to join them, so after the first year they moved out here. The only thing that didn't happen the way I'd spelled it out was the endowment policies. Before we'd got beyond the first one, the local laundry went on the rocks. Well, those girls go through one hell of a lot of laundry. So they bought it and put in a good manager and it started making money again. And rescuing moribund businesses became part of the pattern.'

Keith was none too interested in the financial machinations. 'Wallace,' he said, 'were you – uh – ?'

'None of your damn business,' Wallace said.

'Both of them? At the same time? Tell me the truth or I'll go straight home.'

14

'All right, blast you! Yes, both of them and sometimes together. But I didn't pay them. It was instead of a fee.' Clearly, Wallace felt that this put the relationship into a non-commercial category.

Keith began to revise his opinion of his quiet partner. And yet, for the shy and inhibited Wallace with his terror of women, such a relationship would make a crazy sort of sense. He wondered, momentarily, whether Wallace's stammer dated from that period ...

'I'll tell you this, Keith,' said Wallace. 'Those girls were a revelation to me. I'd always thought that a tart would be an inert lump of meat. But those two could drive a man mad. They could give you a head of steam such as you'd never had before, and only let it blow just before the boiler burst. And then do it all over again. And if they weren't enjoying themselves then they should have been on the stage, except that actresses can't make a tenth of that much money.'

'It's been here all this time and I never knew about it?' Keith said wonderingly.

'You wouldn't,' Wallace said. 'You may be – used to be – the Casanova of southern Scotland, but tarts aren't your scene, you being you.'

'Meaning that I never needed?'

'Meaning that you're too mingy to buy anything you could get for free. But,' Wallace said firmly, 'none of this is what I brought you out here to talk about. The p-point is that the whole thing grew. They could take their pick of the best-looking and most talented girls on the game, who were all beginning to clamour to join in, get away from being dominated by pimps and have an organisation to look after the money for them. And as the word spread that they could offer the very best, and in luxurious surroundings, money began to beat a path to the door.'

'And the health-and-beauty bit?' Keith asked. 'Did that survive?'

'Yes, of course. It had to. First as a legitimate front for the money. But then there were other pressures. Nobody wants flabby girls, so it was natural to put in a couple of tennis courts, then squash and a solarium. And the customers loved the facilities, they could come for some violent exercise, shower, dinner and a

15

girl and g-go home smiling to the wife. So in went more courts, indoor badminton, saunas, exercise room and nine holes of golf. We needed legitimate businesses and profitable uses for capital, so we put in a bar, improved catering, a stock of good wines and a small airstrip. Now there's a swimming-pool on the way. We soon had stockbrokers, or whatever, flying up for the weekend. Exercise and lose a few pounds during the day, dine and enjoy a girl at night. The place is becoming a sort of sensualist's health farm and, Keith, you wouldn't believe what some of them will pay. Not just rich men. There's one oil-rig worker sends his mother a hundred quid as soon as he steps ashore and then comes straight here until he's blown the rest. Then he goes home to mum.'

Keith's curiosity was running along a divergent track. 'But,' he said, 'you told me that they could take the pick of the other girls. How does one girl assess another? A woman's no judge of another woman's sexuality. Do they have a test-pilot? Are you – '

'No I'm bloody well not,' Wallace snapped. 'And just in case you were thinking of applying for the job – '

'I wasn't.'

'– it's taken. And you wouldn't suit. Insufficiently discriminating. Right. I've told you enough about the place. I just wanted you to understand the set-up and not go blundering around saying and doing all the wrong things.'

'I understand all right,' Keith said.

Wallace sighed. 'I don't suppose you do,' he said. 'Just try to remember that this is no back-street bordello. It's a very up-market operation. Very important business conferences happen here, when they want the ultimate in hospitality plus total secrecy. One of the biggest take-overs of the decade was signed in the boardroom. All right, you can drive on now.'

Keith started the car and let it roll forward. 'Does Janet know that her husband – my partner – is accountant to a high-class knocking-shop?'

'Stop the car,' Wallace said. 'Obviously I haven't g-got through to you. One, I am not their accountant; they have one in residence, and two book-keepers. Two, it isn't a knocking-shop; it's a highly respectable group of companies, some of whose

16

property happens to be used for immoral purposes, and they'll sue anybody who suggests otherwise. The Church of Scotland has much the same problem, I believe. Three, Janet knows all about it and thinks it's as funny as hell. She's always wanting the latest gossip.'

Keith let the car roll again. 'Doesn't the resident accountant get a bit distracted at times?' he asked. 'Or is it a woman?'

'It's a man, and he'd better not get distracted. Debbie – the original redhead – retired from the game and married him. She acts as chairman and managing director of the group, and she's damned good at it. But she's a tartar. The other girls know better than to make eyes at her man.'

Keith drove in silence for a while, trying to absorb the overdose of bizarre facts which had been forced on him. 'The operation must have a name,' he said suddenly. 'What's it called?'

'We kept the original name for the house – Millmont House. The group of companies, and most of the individual companies, go under the name of Personal Service. Don't laugh,' Wallace added. 'The name wasn't an exercise in cynical indecency, as you might think. When the girls were in Edinburgh, before the days of the clinic, somebody came to the door doing a household survey. He wanted to know whether the girls worked in industry, commerce, catering or what-have-you, and the only one of his categories which seemed to fit was Personal Service. The name stuck.'

Keith frowned. 'I've seen the names on vans,' he said. 'Laundry, was it?'

'That and a few other things,' Wallace said. 'Turn in here.'

Keith stopped the car. The wrought iron, spike topped gates were set in a high hedge, but he could see that the hedge was backed by barbed wire. A discreet sign said *Millmont House. Clinic.*

Wallace wound down his window. 'Mr James and Mr Calder,' he said. 'We're going to Chalet Sixteen.'

A gruff, Cockney voice spoke, apparently out of the gate-post. 'Morning, Guv,' it said. There was a click at the lock, an electric motor whirred faintly and the gates swung open.

'Neat but not gaudy,' Keith said.

'See what looks like a letter box? There's a closed-circuit television camera in there.'

17

Keith drove forward onto a well-surfaced drive that ran under a canopy of trees. Flowering shrubs, mostly rhododendrons, had been planted so thickly that nowhere was there an uninterrupted view. Keith shook his head. The place was real, but the story, of bullets and supertarts, just had to be a dream or a fantasy on Wallace's part. 'There's been some money spent,' he said tentatively.

'Sprat to catch a mackerel,' Wallace said. 'The girls are coining it.'

'How many are there?'

'Usually between eight and a dozen. I think there are ten or eleven just now, including anybody away on holiday or visiting. They come and go. Retire, or take a few months off to go to the Riviera and look for a rich husband. If they never send for their share of the money, they found one.'

'That happens?'

'It does. We're holding more than twenty thousand for Moira, the other founder-member. Rumour has it she married a Greek shipowner. She doesn't want him to know about her past. But – go left here – if she ever wants the money, we've doubled it for her.'

Keith turned down what might have been a broad path or a very narrow drive, beside a small arrow labelled *sixteen*. Bushes almost scraped the sides of the car. They arrived on an apron of tarmac in front of a cedarboard chalet.

'You have sixteen chalets?' Keith asked as they got out of the car.

'Eighteen. They need spares. Sometimes a guest wants to sleep in, and the girl has another appointment. Sometimes a chalet gets messed up during a party.' Wallace stopped at the front of the door. 'Let us into Sixteen, please, Charlie. Thank you,' he added as the lock clicked.

Although the chalet was the size of a large cottage, it comprised mainly one room, but through two open doors he could see a bathroom and a small but comprehensive kitchenette. The large main room was opulent and, to the surprise of Keith who had been expecting an erotic decor, dignified. He tried not to look at the big water-bed. 'This isn't what I expected,' he said.

Wallace shook his head at the naivety. 'If you were buying sex, would you want to be reminded of the transaction? Or would you rather be able to imagine that you were seducing a duchess? Leave the door open so that we don't have to call Charlie up to get out again. And don't raise your voice or you'll activate the cameras and microphones.'

Keith had been expecting the sleazy side to surface. 'Huh!' he said. 'Space-age equivalent of the *cabinet de voyeur?*'

'It's the space-age equivalent of having someone outside the door, just in case the customer decides that it might be fun to rough the girl up a little. There's a rota of very tough nuts on porter duty. And the knowledge that you can't get out unless the girl clears it with the porter makes quite a deterrent.'

Two

The back wall of the room was lined with a single panel, veneered in some pale timber – sycamore, Keith thought. On it was arranged a collection of what Keith at first supposed to be reproduction antique guns. He was drawn towards them, pointing like a gundog. Each one was an original.

'Where in God's name did you get this lot?' Keith asked. He gave a low whistle. 'I've been looking for a Ferguson Rifle for years. Even the one in Edinburgh Castle's only a sporting copy.'

'One of our customers was raising money in a hurry. You're always telling me they're a good investment, and good investments are always needed here. We paid him just over eight thousand for them.'

'Would you take a hundred per cent profit?'

'We'll hang onto them for the moment, thanks. Could any of these have fired that ball?'

The light of enthusiasm faded in Keith's eye. The expert in him took over. The guns were fixed flat to the wall, partly by a hook in each barrel, and he could not get his gauge into use; but years of practice had taught him to estimate the diameter of a bore to within a very small margin. He worked his way through the collection, muttering aloud. 'Too small ... smoothbore ... unserviceable (let me have it for a day or two) ... too small ... too large ... I repaired this one for you, didn't I?'

'You did.'

'You told me it belonged to your old mother. I didn't know she was on the game.'

'I could hardly tell you the truth.'

'I gave you a special price,' Keith said sadly. 'Why aren't there any ramrods?'

'Too easily pinched as souvenirs. I've got them all locked up safely.'

'Uhuh.' Keith finished his inspection. 'This duelling pistol, now. Saw-handled. Possibly Boutet of Versailles. One of a pair. Pity you don't have the other. Started as flintlock and some bloody vandal converted it to percussion by barrel-nipple in about 1840. I could convert it back to flintlock for you.'

'That would make it more valuable?' Wallace asked.

'Much more. Anyway, this could be the culprit. It's been cleaned, but it smells of fresh gun-oil and black powder smoke.'

'G-goddam!' Wallace said. 'I was hoping you'd clear them all. How would he get it off the wall? Those hooks aren't screwed on, they're bolted right through.'

Keith laughed in a way that Wallace thought maddeningly superior. 'You should have consulted me about security. A hook in the barrel and another through the trigger-guard's all very well, but we could have done better. Look, I'll show you something.' Keith pointed to a beautifully engraved and inlaid Queen Anne pistol. 'Whoever it was, he tried to get this one down. See how he's used a screwdriver on what he thought were screw-heads and burred them? He could have loaded that one from the breech end, and with a flintlock he wouldn't have had problems getting a matching percussion-cap. He couldn't get it down, so he switched his attention to the other one. The trigger-guard on the Queen Anne fixes from inside and he'd have had to dismantle the whole pistol to get it off the wall. So he took two screws out of the Boutet, turned the trigger-guard and lifted the pistol down. Then afterwards, I suppose to try and cover some of his tracks, he cleaned it and reversed the process. It's in an awkward position, and the screws aren't quite home.'

Wallace looked for himself, and grunted. The signs were to be seen, if you knew where to look.

Keith produced his own tools, unscrewed the trigger-guard and took down the pistol again. 'Like that,' he said. He took his gauge out of its long case and measured the bore. 'Hard to tell exactly,' he said, 'because it's both swamped and belled, but I make it about point six one five at its tightest. That'd just about take the ball with a cloth patch. Let's have a look at the chair.'

'They took it up to the house.'

'They shouldn't muck about at the scene of a crime.'

'Well, you just did,' Wallace pointed out. 'Except that we don't know for sure that there's been a crime.'

'Pull your head out of the sand, ostrich,' Keith said, 'and show me where the chair stood when it was noticed.'

A single leather armchair with a cushion of tartan tweed stood facing the stone fireplace. Wallace moved it round so that it stood to one side of the fireplace with its back to the door. 'This was here,' he said. 'The one with the blood was opposite.'

Keith sat down in the real chair and stared at a mental image of the other. His posture became fixed, his eyes staring unseeingly at the far wall, always his attitude when deep in thought. Eventually, he stirred. Wallace waited expectantly.

'I'm hungry,' Keith said.

Wallace looked at his watch. 'We've missed lunch.' He raised his voice. 'Hoy! Charlie!'

There was a faint hum as the audio system came to life. The same gruff voice came over a hidden speaker. 'Yes, Mr James?'

Wallace looked at the mirror over the fireplace. 'Could you send us down some sandwiches – smoked salmon – and a bottle of the *Liebfraumilch,* please?'

'Make mine a pint of Guinness,' Keith said.

'Right you are, Guv.' The hum snapped off.

Keith nodded at the mirror. 'That's where the camera is?'

'That's it.'

'Humph. Take a look at the furniture, fitments and walls.'

'What am I looking for?'

Keith produced the lead ball from his ticket-pocket and showed Wallace the mark. 'A slot like that,' he said, 'made by a screwdriver. He won't have used the floor. Wrong way up.'

'Of course,' Wallace said sardonically, but he got to work. Keith, if questioned when trying to concentrate, was inclined unwittingly to become more rather than less obscure.

Keith himself went down on his knees. He studied the seat and arms of the chair, and then began a minute examination of the deep-pile carpet. 'Seems very clean,' he said. 'Has it been vacuumed since then?'

'Since when?' said Wallace.

'I see what you mean.'

The food had still not arrived by the time that Wallace had exhausted the possibilities of the walls and furniture. Keith had

22

finished with the carpet and was studying the contents of the vacuum-cleaner. At last a car drew up outside, a door closed and a squat shadow filled the doorway. A burly man with no neck, no hair and almost no nose brought in a laden tray.

'Oh, it's you, Charlie,' Wallace said. 'Should you be away from the desk?'

'Doris is covering for me, Guv. Sorry I was so long, but I 'ad to go down to the village for the Guinness.'

Keith looked up from his small pile of dust and fluff. 'You're not as big as I expected,' he said.

'They don't need to be giants,' Wallace said defensively.

'You used to wrestle as Charlie Fairweather,' Keith said. 'I saw you a few times at Leith Baths, and at the Caird Hall.'

'Did you now?' Charlie put the tray down. He shuffled his feet. 'Fairweather's me own name. But I was the Masked Marauder, too.'

'Were you, though? You looked taller in the ring.'

'That's the way it is,' Charlie said. 'Well, cheers. Ta for now!' He bustled out and they heard the car drive off.

'Salt of the earth,' Wallace said, 'and a pillar of this establishment, but I wish he'd stick to his own damned job. It's just his eternal curiosity that brought him down here. Well, what do you make of it?'

Keith took the only chair and helped himself to a sandwich. Wallace settled himself on the end of the water-bed, bobbing gently up and down. 'It doesn't add up yet,' Keith said. 'Can I take it that you don't keep black powder on the premises?'

'You certainly can.'

'Who cleans the chalets?'

'The girls do their own cleaning, change the linen and so on. It's their only other duty.'

'Yes. It wouldn't do to have an army of daily cleaners wandering around. I want to see the chair, and I'd like to meet the girl who – er – usually occupies this chalet.'

'Can do,' Wallace said. He clapped his hands. 'Hoy!'

The speakers came alive. A woman's voice said, 'Yes, Mr James?'

'Ask Mrs Heller to speak, if she's free, please, Doris.'

23

'I'll see.'

Keith took another sandwich. 'These are good,' he said.

'Nothing but the best around here.'

Another voice came over the speakers, musical and, for a woman's voice, deep. The Kensington accent was so good that Keith nearly missed the faint underlying trace of Glasgow. 'Hullo, Wal,' it said. 'Has the mystery been solved?'

'Not yet. We'd like to see the chair, and have a word with Hilary if she isn't – er – doing anything.'

'Or anybody,' the voice said with a tremor of laughter. 'I'll arrange it. Come up in about half an hour. Is that your friend? I can only see the top of his head ...' Keith leaned away from the mirror. 'Thank you. Isn't he good-looking.' Keith leaned back towards the fireplace, hurriedly. That kind of comment from that kind of person made him nervous.

There was a faint click as the audio system switched off. 'You mustn't mind her,' Wallace said. 'She just can't break the habit. Do you want the last sandwich?'

'I do, but you can have it.' Keith drained his glass. 'Remind me to find out which pub this came from – they keep it well. Now, I want to look over the rest of the place.'

The bathroom was just a luxurious bathroom with bidet and shower. The cosmetics and bath-salts seemed to be of high quality in wholesale packs. The kitchenette was well-stocked with convenience meals of luxury standard. In the main room, one cupboard held an excellent selection of wines and spirits, and a miniature safe with a slot-shaped opening in the top. Another cupboard was almost filled with clothing, and contained a laundry basket that was more than half full. 'The laundry bill must be astronomic,' Keith said.

'It was, until we bought the laundry.'

'You should own a lingerie factory as well.'

'They do.'

Keith flipped through the contents of a third cupboard, which were personal to the usual occupant of the chalet and therefore of no interest. Or so Keith thought.

There was little in the chalet to indicate its usual purpose. The hard-core cassettes racked beside the television set and its accompanying video-recorder could, he decided, have been matched in many private houses. Beside the bed was an expensive transistor radio in an alligator-skin case.

As they went out, he looked at the door. It had no keyholes at all. They pulled it shut behind them. 'Leave the car here,' Wallace said. 'It's as easy to walk.'

Their path, which was too narrow for a car, led through the ubiquitous shrubs. The planting, Wallace explained, had been one of the attractions of the estate, but even so had been added to over the years. 'Most clients prefer complete privacy,' he said. They crossed another side-drive. A discreet marker pointed to Chalet Fifteen, another to Tennis Court Three. Through the trees, Keith glimpsed the court where two girls were locked in grim battle. The standard of tennis looked very high.

'As I said, men like fit girls, not fat girls.'

'Tell me about the girl in Chalet Sixteen,' Keith said.

'Hilary? Her real name's Morag, or something like that. Comes from the West Highlands somewhere.'

'That's unusual, isn't it?' Keith asked.

'I think it is. I get the picture of a girl reacting against an over-strict upbringing. Blonde.'

'In other words, you don't know a damn thing about her?'

'Not a lot,' Wallace said.

Nearer the house a J.C.B. was working on a large excavation. 'Swimming-pool,' Wallace said. 'They'll put a roof over it next year. Well, it all adds to the value of the property.'

The house was some Victorian baron's vision of Scottish vernacular architecture, all stone with crow-stepped gables and occasional turrets, but it was well proportioned and in very good order. Their approach led past a yard where a dozen cars stood, mostly of models far beyond what he would ever be able to afford. 'They have this many clients so early on a Tuesday?' Keith asked.

Wallace paused and looked. 'The Rolls is a client,' he said. 'Must be left over from last night. The Mini belongs to Lord . . . well, I won't tell you his name. He's almost permanently resident here.

25

The family pays all the bills, just as long as he stays well out of their way. The rest of the cars belong to the girls. They don't take them down to the chalets. It puts the clients off to see another car already outside the door.' They walked on. 'Most of the pocket-money goes on cars and jewelery,' Wallace said. 'And clothes. Then they can take days off and go on the hunt. A good-looking girl in tweed and pearls and a Ferrari, going to the races or the golf on her own, has a damn good chance of taking up with a rich man, even a rich husband. You'd be amazed how many men have no idea of their wife's past history.'

Keith thought. No, he knew all about Molly's past.

In the hall behind the classical entrance, at a desk dwarfed by mahogany panelling and vast oil-portraits of fierce looking gentlemen, the porter was using a carefully correct voice to the telephone while punching the keys on a small console and at the same time watching a high-level video-screen. Beside him stood a battery of television monitors, all of them blank. 'Miss Lillian will be pleased to receive you at nine-thirty,' he said. 'Chalet Seven. Thank *you*.'

'You've got a *computer*?' Keith said incredulously.

'Best way to keep track of who's to be where when,' Wallace said. 'It's only a mini, and it's leased.'

'You don't have to explain it to me,' Keith said. He saw that a small dining-room and a smaller bar led off the hall. 'I was trying to think what this place reminded me of. It's like the better sort of man's club.'

One of the monitors flickered on. A girl whose beauty was entirely on display was crossing her room, quite unaware of the intrusion of male eyes. Charlie, the porter, touched a switch. 'Summink wrong, Miss Ursula?'

The girl was unperturbed. 'For Christ's sake, Charlie,' she said, 'I only farted.' Her voice could only have been Cheltenham-and-Girton.

'No you never,' Charlie retorted. He made a note in a big diary. 'You slammed the bathroom door. If you could fart loud enough to throw the switch you'd be on *real* television. An' you better get a move on. If your next gentleman's on time, you've got six minutes.' He switched the system off and winked. 'Farted, indeed! Mind you, I could have believed it of some of the others.'

26

When Debbie Heller came to the door of her office behind the reception desk, Keith was in no doubt about her identity. Her red-gold hair was as Wallace had described it, and her deep, musical voice was as he remembered – almost perfect, but marred by a vestige of Glasgow's glottal stops. (He could be sure now, with the real thing fresh in his ears.) She added up to a woman of overpowering but apparently unconscious sexuality. Her face was soft but her eyes were observant and very sharp. She gave Keith's hand a lingering shake, and kissed Wallace on the lips. 'Hilary will be here in ten minutes,' she said. She sounded positive.

Her office was elegant, sober and respectable as the rest of the place. The chair in the middle of the haircord carpet was the twin of the other except for a matching tartan chairback or anti-macassar which Keith lifted off. Underneath, the leather was palely stained.

'He tried to wipe it off,' Keith said, 'but somebody lost a hell of a lot of blood. You'd better call the cops.'

She locked eyes with him. She reminded him of a girl he had once known. No, that was wrong. She reminded him of every girl that he had ever known. 'Not yet,' she said. 'An hour or two can't matter. Give us your conclusion first.'

'You're wasting time.'

'I'll pay you for yours.'

Keith shrugged, and saw Wallace watching him with malicious amusement. 'All right,' Keith said. 'But we're only duplicating what they'll do again and better.'

He knelt down and probed the hole in the chair's high back. The style was old but the construction modern, and he kept pulling out shreds of foamed plastic. As he worked he could hear Wallace describing their researches in Chalet Sixteen. 'There's no patch in here,' he said at last, sitting back on his heels. 'That's a small wrapping, to make the ball a tight fit in the barrel. It must have stayed in the wound. Or he could have recovered it afterwards. He probably ripped up his own handkerchief. I take it that you haven't found a hole cut out of a curtain or such?'

'Now, Wal, you sit down.' Wallace sank into the chair with a certain reluctance. 'You're average size,' Keith said, 'or slightly above. On the safeish assumption that the victim was neither a

27

giant nor a dwarf and was firmly seated at the time, the shot went through his neck. From the blood, it seems to have hit one of the big blood-vessels. My guess would be that he'd be unconscious from that moment, and dead in less than half a minute.'

'The neck's a poor sort of target,' Wallace said. 'And you'd expect him to aim where there'd be the least blood spilled.'

'If he aimed for it. He may have meant to shoot for the head, and squeezed the pistol with his whole hand, as he might with a shotgun, instead of just using the trigger finger. That'd make him shoot low.'

Keith, for some reason of his own, was examining the chair's wooden arms when a knock, timid and respectful, came at the door. Mrs Heller called to come in.

The newcomer was a brown-eyed blonde, tall and tanned, dressed, Keith thought, for attending the grouse moors by Bentley rather than for amorous commerce. Her face was pleasing but unremarkable. Her figure, in conformity with the local mode, was delicious; and her voice, like Mrs Heller's, was almost perfect, the only perceptible trace of her origins being a gentle, euphonious cadence that suggested to Keith, as it had to Wallace, the Western Highlands. Keith held a chair for her, and she looked at Mrs Heller before she accepted it.

Mrs Heller sat down behind her desk. It was a big desk, almost bare of papers, but it confronted two big video-screens. 'Tell us all you know about the chair,' she said. 'In fact, tell us all about Sunday evening.'

Miss Hilary moistened her lips and gripped her alligator hand-bag until her knuckles whitened. She started to speak, and paused to clear her throat. Keith thought that she was scared of Mrs Heller, and not without reason. Keith was beginning to appreciate that under a girlish shell was a formidable lady. 'I'd had a visitor in the afternoon,' she said. 'As I told you, I think everything was all right then. At seven, I was with Annette in Chalet Fifteen. We had two gentlemen, and they ordered dinner down from the kitchen. They had two bottles of claret with dinner, but, honestly, Annette and I only had a glass each.' She paused.

Evidently, Mrs Heller was adept at reading the signs. 'What else?' she asked ominously.

'The men smoked a little pot. *Leis an fhirinn innseadh.*' she added hastily, lapsing for a moment in her anxiety, 'I took only one puff, just to be sociable. Truly.'

Mrs Heller looked severely at her. 'You know I don't like the girls to indulge,' she said. 'They didn't get it from you?'

'No.' Miss Hilary looked terrified. 'Definitely not.'

'All right, then. What next?'

'I took my one back to Number Sixteen. He called himself Don Donaldson, but that's not his real name. You can tell, when they're slow to answer. I think he had a good time,' she added modestly.

'Anything unusual?'

'No. He was straight.'

Mrs Heller sighed. 'I didn't mean in bed. Did anything unusual happen?'

'Nothing at all. He thanked me politely and asked if he might stay and doze until his friend was ready. Well, I'd had his friend before, and he's a slow starter. I had a late appointment – a musician who sometimes comes after the clubs shut, if he's in the money. So I spoke to Bert, and Bert said to use Chalet Four, and I did, and I stayed there all night.'

'And yesterday?'

'I had a three o'clock appointment and I'd slept a bit late. I cleaned up in Number Four, came up here for an early lunch in the dining room and went back to Sixteen. I changed the sheets and dusted out and so on, and I was just away to take my shower and get prettied up when I noticed that the cloth was missing off one of the chairbacks. I thought that maybe Donaldson had taken it as a souvenir, some of them do the damnedest things. The other one was a wee bit –'

'A little bit,' Mrs Heller said.

'– a little bit greasy, so I lifted it off to take up to the house-keeper and get two clean ones. I saw the stains and the hole so I called Peter and he came and took the chair away and I was just ready in time for my visitor,' she finished breathlessly.

'Number Fifteen's usually empty,' Mrs Heller said. 'Why did you use it on Sunday?'

'Bert told us to. Annette said that she had another appointment just before, and she mightn't have time to tidy up. We needed two chalets. Bert said to use Fifteen.'

Mrs Heller raised her eyebrows at Keith and then at Wallace.

'When you got back to Sixteen on Monday,' Keith said, 'was the door shut?'

The girl nodded emphatically. 'Peter had to let me in. It'll be in the book.'

'Did you notice a smell?'

'Cigarette smoke. Don must have smoked two, because there were two stubs in the ash-tray. Tobacco, not pot. I left the door open and put the fans on while I tidied up.'

'And you're absolutely sure that both cloths were on the chairs the day before?' Keith asked.

Miss Hilary looked at him with gentle reproach in her cow-like brown eyes. 'I've already told you so. I always straighten them when I tidy the room, and I always straighten the room after a visitor, and I'd had a visitor during the afternoon.' She turned to Mrs Heller. 'It was the gentleman whose wife always pays for a visit here on his birthday.'

Mrs Heller raised her eyebrows again. Keith shook his head. 'All right,' she said. 'Wait outside. No, on second thoughts, when's your next appointment?'

'Not until this evening. Tuesday's always quiet.'

'Then go downstairs to the hairdresser. Get your hair done. Your parting's beginning to show. After that, be available. And keep your mouth tight shut.'

'Yes, Mrs Heller.' Keith could have sworn that, on her way out, the girl almost curtseyed.

Debbie Heller looked at Keith. 'Well?' she said. 'What do we do now?'

'Either you call the police, or you forget it.'

'Tell me why.'

'Because you still can't be sure, and while you aren't sure you can still pretend it never happened. You see, there are two possibilities. One, somebody was shot.'

'And two?'

'Two, somebody wants you out of business. Could that be to anyone's advantage?'

Mrs Heller frowned, creasing an otherwise lovely brow. 'Yes,' she said, 'it could. You mean we're being framed?'

'It's possible. The girl, Hilary, couldn't have mistaken black-powder-smoke for cigarette smoke. The carpet didn't seem to be stained. And your microphone system would surely have come on.'

'What do you think happened, then?'

'I don't think it happened,' Keith said patiently. 'I'm just offering you your last excuse to forget the whole thing. Suppose that somebody with the necessary skills drew off a pint of his own blood, or somebody else's for that matter. In digging out the ball, you spoiled any chance of proving whether it was shot into the chair or pushed in through a stab-hole, and I made it worse probing for the patch. Suppose he splashed the blood around and mopped it up again, pinched one of your chair-back things, and beat it.'

For the first time, Debbie Heller smiled. Keith could well see what Wallace might once have seen in her. 'I like it,' she said.

'Don't get to like it too much,' said Keith.

'Why not? It fits the known facts and explains the missing ones.'

Wallace, who had sat quietly in the background, decided to speak up. 'Because the police haven't arrived yet. That's what you mean, isn't it Keith?'

Mrs Heller pursed her lips. The smile was quite gone. 'You mean, there was no point in framing us unless the fuzz were tipped off? So he could be giving us a day or two to incriminate ourselves? I don't think I like that thought very much. Yet your friend thinks there's a doubt . . .'

'I think there's room for doubt as to whether anyone was shot in that chalet. Are you sure you want to know any more? You could still get rid of the chair and forget it.'

'I wish that we could, but we can't.' It was as if the attractive young woman had never been. Her eyes were hard and sharp, her manner decisive. She was a sexless decision-maker packaged in a chocolate-box shell. 'If somebody's out to get us we need to know. And if there was a murder, a fatal accident or a suicide on our premises which somebody tried to cover up, I want to know it. Murder seems the most likely, and I could neither condone it nor take the risk of covering it up.'

31

Keith nodded. He could have bowed, and she knew it. 'Is the same type of chair in general use?'

'Yes.'

'And the colour of the tweed?'

'The same,' she said. 'It makes for easier housekeeping.'

'Then,' Keith said, 'we'd better think some more. I never could picture your client taking down the pistol, loading it and then waiting for somebody to come in and sit down. But if he were going after somebody else, it makes sense. He loads the pistol, walks to another chalet and does the deed. He doesn't want a hue and cry. So he covers up his traces, and those that he can't he scatters around so that the explanation is harder and later to arrive at. He swaps the chairs between the chalets, mops up the blood with the tweed cover that has the hole in it, and bungs it with the body into the boot of his car.'

'Two theories,' Mrs Heller said. 'And apart from the non-arrival of the police, not an Israeli foreskin to choose between them. Or is there some evidence I don't know about yet?'

'I'm afraid there is,' Keith said. 'I held it back to give you a chance to back out with a clear conscience. Take a look at the back of the chair.' He showed them the outline of what seemed to be a faint shadow down the side of the chair. 'If you stand back and look at it,' he said, 'it seems to outline where the tweed cloth and the man's shoulder might have been. It's almost certainly part of the pattern of burned gunpowder particles.'

'Oh dear,' Mrs Heller said mildy. 'So there was a shot. And if there was a shot, the whole thing isn't a frame-up?' She pressed a switch on the small console on her desk. 'Charlie, I want the log-book for Sunday and a print-out of appointments for the same period. Pronto.'

'Yerse, mum,' came Charlie's voice.

Within a few minutes he brought in a ledger-like tome and a folded sheet of print-out. 'Will you be long with the diary, mum?' he asked. 'We need it.'

'Start another one.'

As the door closed behind Charlie, Keith got to his feet. 'Can I see that?'

She closed the ledger on the print-out. 'No you bloody well

32

can't,' she said. 'Sit down where you are. We'd lose ninety per cent of our clients if we weren't absolutely confidential.'

Keith resumed his seat. 'Yes, mum,' he said. He turned to Wallace, who was looking slightly shocked at this *lèse-majesté*. 'Are the real identities of the clients known?' he asked.

'Some,' Wallace said. 'Losh, some of them pay by cheque or credit card. Some want a quarterly account to their homes. But a majority use false names and pay cash.'

Mrs Heller looked up from the print-out. 'We often do know who they are,' she said. 'Emergency phone calls. Lost property. Photographs in newspapers. We never let on that we know. One M.P. still thinks we think his name's Blenkinsop. Right!' She closed the book, locked it with the print-out in a drawer of her desk and spoke from memory. 'The man in Number Sixteen called himself Don Donaldson. Hilary didn't know him and I don't recognise the name. Probably it was his first time here, but I'll have a check made on the name. It could even be real.

'The reservations were made by the other man. He called himself Harold Fosdyke. That won't be real. Some of them pick oddball names because they're easier to remember. Fosdyke stayed with Annette in Fifteen. Both girls had other appointments, so that Donaldson and Fosdyke were left in Sixteen and Fifteen respectively, to recover,' this was said without the least expression, 'and to leave in their own good time.'

'Now comes the bit that I don't like much. The two men arrived together by car. There was only one man in the car when it left.'

Wallace winced and Keith pursed his lips in a silent whistle. 'Has Chalet Fifteen been cleaned yet?' Keith asked.

'It should have been,' Mrs Heller said, 'but I doubt it. The girls are supposed to tidy up after every visitor, but there isn't always time. Annette went off next morning with another girl, to act as hostesses for a week on some industrialist's yacht. Hilary should have tidied up, but she's a lazy monkey at times and I don't suppose she bothered. You two can go and take a look.'

'You're not coming?' Keith asked.

'I've got more to do with my time. Come back and tell me all about it later.' She glanced out of the window. 'Is that your car opposite the front door?'

33

'No,' Keith said. 'Don't you want cars parked there?'

'I don't give a hoot where you park, but if you leave a car under that tree the little birdies'll crap all over it.'

As they went through the hall, Charlie, the porter, was speaking into his microphone. 'Miss Lynn to Chalet Twelve, please. Your visitor is on the way. Miss Lynn to Chalet Twelve.'

They retraced their steps past the yard, past the excavation for the swimming-pool. As they came within sight of the now deserted tennis court Keith said, 'This place seems better organised than most car plants.'

'So it should,' Wallace said. 'I taught them myself.'

'You mean my respected partner's management consultant to a whorehouse?'

'Was,' Wallace said. 'Was.'

'Was respected?'

'Was consultant. I set up most of the administration, but Debbie caught on amazingly. Inside a fluffy-minded scrubber there was a born manager-accountant screaming to get out.'

'She seems hard on the girls. Women can't always cope with power.'

'Don't let her fool you. If one of the girls is in trouble, Debbie'll fight like a tigress for her. Out of business, they're her friends. In the boardroom, they're fellow-directors. But in that room they're employees, and they'd better not forget it.' They turned off their previous path. 'Oh God!' Wallace said. 'I don't think that I want to know any more.'

'Mrs Heller wants us to investigate.'

'And what Debbie wants, Debbie gets. Sometimes I worry about what I've done to that girl, turning her from a tart bubbling with fun and affection into a sort of animated computer. Makes me feel Svengalish.' They stopped outside Chalet Fifteen and Wallace spoke into the hidden microphone. 'Let us into Fifteen, Charlie, please.'

The lock clicked. They pushed the door open. 'Shit!' Wallace said. 'I was hoping it'd all turn out to be a bad dream.'

Three

Back in Debbie Heller's office the atmosphere, despite the solace of tea and biscuits, was far from convivial. Mrs Heller had the ledger and print-out open on her desk again, and sat poised, calm and in control. Hilary, her hair wrapped in a towel, sat nervously on the edge of her chair and tried not to fidget. Wallace looked as if he wished himself far, far away.

Keith used the voice which he reserved for telling a customer that his gun was beyond repair or had failed proof. 'I'm afraid there's no doubt about it at all,' he said. 'The smell of black-powder-smoke was still hanging on the air. And there had been blood spilled. The chair must have stood close to the fireplace; the tiles have been wiped over, but you can still see pink traces in the joints. And where the back of the chair would have been, the carpet's still damp.'

Mrs Heller's face remained calm but her fingers made the papers rustle. 'It could still be a frame,' she suggested, 'but more elaborate than you thought.'

'I found some fragments of a percussion-cap,' Keith said. 'The evidence is piling up. I think you've got to call the fuzz.'

'Not yet,' Mrs Heller said. She met Wallace's eye for a moment. 'If we run over it from the beginning, putting in all that we know or can infer, we may get a better picture.' She looked down and compared the print-out with the log-book. 'I'll make a start. On Wednesday of last week there was a phone call from the man who called himself Fosdyke. He had been here seven time in the past two years, never on his own. The staff think that he's a fixer, entertaining potential buyers or clients, or buying some influence. Nobody recognised any of his companions, but the general impression was of men of a certain status.'

'Is there any record of who introduced him?' Keith asked.

'None. And no clue to his real name or identity. He asked for an appointment for himself and a friend for Saturday evening. That was impossible – we were busy as a Gorbals pub on the first night of Glasgow Fair – so he accepted a booking for Sunday.'

'Did he ask for particular girls?'

'He asked for Hilary by name for his friend'(Hilary put her hand up as if to touch at her hair) 'but said that he himself would take his chance. "Pot-luck" he called it. It seems to have been purest chance that he got Annette. Their appointment was for seven p.m. They arrived at the gate at six fifty-four.'

'Any car number?'

Mrs Heller shook her red-gold head regretfully. 'White Granada estate, that's all we know. Now, Hilary.'

Miss Hilary sat up straight in front of the headmistress, gripping her alligator bag for comfort. 'I went to Number Fifteen early, to be sure it was tidy,' she said virtuously. 'The men arrived about seven and Annette was a minute or two behind them. They'd ordered dinner for four over the phone, and Bert brought it down.'

'Just a moment,' Mrs Heller said. 'You were first at Number Fifteen. Was it all spick and span?'

'Absolutely.'

'Did Bert let you in?'

Hilary's mouth made a pink O while she thought. 'It was Bert,' she said at last. 'But I heard old Lucy's voice when she let Bert in with the dinner. We left the door open after that, because it was so hot in the chalets.'

'Any drinking before dinner?' Keith asked.

'The men had a dram or two. I just took a tonic water.' For the first time, Hilary began to look animated. 'For dinner, we had –'

'That's all in the record,' Mrs Heller said firmly.

Hilary subsided. 'It's just that I hadn't had any lunch,' she said, 'being busy.'

'Would you say that the men were sober?' Keith asked.

'Not to say sober, nor drunk either. Just drink taken, and they'd blown some pot. They were in control of their bodies,' Hilary said judiciously, 'but their minds were beginning to fly – my one more than Annette's.'

'Describe them,' Mrs Heller said.

Hilary looked surprised. She saw many men, without ever really looking at them. 'Annette's one, Mr Fosdyke, he's big and

36

heavy, with a pot on him and lots of muscle. Like I said –'

'*As* you said.'

'As I said, I've met him before. He's . . . not very nice. Do you want to know –?'

'I don't think it's relevant at the moment,' Mrs Heller said. 'Go on describing him.'

Hilary thought hard. She seemed to feel that she had described everything that she could be expected to notice. 'He had sandy hair, and little sandy curls all over him. And a snub nose,' she finished triumphantly.

'And the other one?'

'Smaller. Quite light, really. He was nice. Polite and considerate.'

'But what did he look like?' Mrs Heller demanded.

'I only met him the once.'

The others uttered a collective sigh. 'You'd be hurt,' Keith said, 'if he couldn't remember your face.'

'He'd be more likely to remember the back of my neck,' Hilary said.

Mrs Heller put on a pair of glasses, thickly horn-rimmed, and looked at Hilary over the top of them. 'That kind of remark is not funny,' she said severely. Hilary quailed. 'Go on with the story of the evening.'

'We finished dinner about eight,' Hilary said in a subdued voice. 'Mr Fosdyke was getting amorous, so Don and I split off. We went to Sixteen. He was all done in a few minutes and he couldn't get started again, so we just dozed off on the bed until Bert called me just after nine-thirty to remind me about my next appointment. I'd just showered and dressed when he called again to say that my next gentleman was at the gate. I said that Mr Donaldson was still with me in Sixteen, and Don sort of groaned that he wanted to rest a bit, so Bert said to go to Number Four. Bert worked the door for me, and Don said to leave it open because he was hot. He was snoring his head off in the chair before I was even out of the door. I can't think of anything else. And, please, my hair's not finished and I've got an appointment soon.' She sounded almost tearful.

'All right,' Mrs Heller said. 'You can go for now. Remember, not a word to anybody or you'll catch it from me.' She watched the girl to the door. 'You're putting on weight,' she said suddenly. 'Do you want me to put you on a crash diet?'

The girl shook her head dumbly.

'Then cut down and get some exercise. Play tennis with Dawn – she's developing a bum like an elephant and you can tell her I said so. Out!'

The door closed very gently against a sigh of relief.

Debbie Heller pushed her glasses back up her nose. They made her look very young, but there was nothing of youth in the calm assurance of her manner. 'I'll have an abstract made of the entries that could be relevant,' she said. 'But so far they seem to check out, at least as far as doors are concerned. The trouble is that although we could usually check anybody's movements by the need to have doors opened, that happened less than usual on that night.'

'Because it was a hot night?' Keith asked.

'Yes. And the fans make rather a noise.'

'So they closed doors if they were about to – er – sing a few rousing choruses of "I used to kiss you on the lips, but it's all over now",' Keith said delicately, 'but otherwise doors were left open?'

'Exactly. However, there's one entry that bugs me. It's in Bert's writing – he was on until midnight. He starts with a star – that's the symbol for the system being triggered by a noise. It takes half a second for the system to warm up, so if it's a short noise you don't hear it. The entry reads, "No 15 Man. Says let door slam". That's all.'

'Terse,' Keith said.

'It is. But,' Mrs Heller said, 'in all fairness, the log's mainly kept as a check on customer's accounts. If the audio system gets triggered and the reason seems harmless, a very brief entry's quite acceptable. But it's timed 10.21, and there's no record of the man asking for the door to be opened again. The white Granada left before midnight.'

'It c-could have been the bathroom door,' Wallace said.

'Note the wording,' Mrs Heller said. "Man. Says let door slam". Says. The bathroom and kitchen doors are in full view of the camera. The outside door isn't. Nor is the position where you say the chair was. So if there was a shooting, it was at 10.21.'

38

'I don't want to say "I told you so",' Keith said, 'but I told you so. You've got to call the police. It fits together too neatly. Two men arrive, dine with the two girls and separate to two chalets. The girls have other engagements and move on, leaving the men to recover. The men were half-pissed and had been smoking pot.

'It's possible but unlikely that one of the men left and was replaced by somebody we don't know about. But, to keep it simple, let's assume that the action's confined to the same duo.

'One of them, probably the man in Chalet Sixteen, decides that he needs a weapon. Maybe it was a delusion stoked by drink and pot – in that sort of a state, a man can get his motives muddled and still be competent to handle physical problems. On the wall of Chalet Sixteen he sees a whole lot of antique but workable guns. From somewhere he produces powder, ball and a percussion cap. You tell me that nothing like that's kept around here, but you could check on your staff's hobbies. More likely, one man or the other was an enthusiast for muzzle-loading guns, and there was gear in the car.

'He was trying for a pistol which could take a lead ball that he had with him. He tried first for the Queen Anne flintlock, which wouldn't even have needed a percussion cap, but he couldn't get it off the wall. So he settled for the duelling pistol.'

'Do people really still shoot those things?' Mrs Heller asked.

'Good Lord, yes. A muckle part of the shop's business is built around muzzle-loaders. Originals and reproductions, flintlock and percussion. And the accessories. Flasks, horns and pouches, bullet-moulds and so on. They have something on at Bisley almost every month, and clay pigeon events, local challenge trophies, inter-club challenge matches and the lot.'

'Sorry I asked.' She smiled disarmingly. 'Go on about what happened.'

'He loaded the pistol. And here's where we begin to pick up wee crottles of evidence. He didn't have the ramrod, because Wal keeps them locked up against souvenir hunters. You can't push the ball down easily with a screwdriver – the ball tends to roll and the blade jams against the wall of the barrel. So he used the handle end. You can see the marks of the screwdriver blade under the arm of a chair in Number Fifteen. That must have been the chair that he swapped over. You can also see the mark of the blade on the ball, which would've been him giving it a last push after it was seated.

'Next, he needed a percussion-cap.' Keith noticed that Debbie Heller was looking dazed. Trying to keep from his voice any suggestion of Listen With Mother, he went into more detail. 'That pistol, you'll understand, dates from after the flintlock era but before the arrival of the breech-loading gun with cartridges. It was still muzzle-loaded, but to set it off there was a copper cap on a nipple, to be struck by the hammer.' Keith nearly apologised for the word nipple, but remembered where he was. 'The nipple on that pistol would take a twenty-six cap, which is in common use but not universal.

'I thought he'd be damn lucky to find a pistol in that collection which could take both the ball and the cap that he had available. And I'd noticed a trace of sticky guck around the nipple. So I had a hunt around the floor of Number Fifteen, and sure enough I found some fragments of copper. Those caps are only too prone to fly to bits at the best of times, and I guessed that a misfitting cap would be almost a certainty.' Keith tipped some fragments of copper out of a twist of paper.

Wallace bent over them. 'Chewing-gum?' he suggested.

Keith looked at Mrs Heller. 'Does Hilary chew gum?' he asked.

She waved a vague hand. 'It hardly matters. The bedside table in each chalet's kept stocked with everything a man could suddenly want, from paper tissues to cough-drops. Including chewing-gum.'

'Right,' Keith said. He poked at the metal fragments with a matchstick. 'There's a number of sizes of nipple, and caps to match. Generally speaking, the bigger the gun the bigger the cap. These bits were certainly never a twenty-six. More like a "military top hat". It's called that because of the shape,' he explained.

'I had sort of guessed that,' Mrs Heller said. 'Let's hear the rest of it.'

'There's not a lot more to say. He stuck the too-big cap onto the too-small nipple with chewing-gum, and he walked from Number Sixteen to Number Fifteen. We don't know whether he wanted the pistol for defence or offence, or whether he intended to commit a hold-up or whether he was doped to the eyebrows and hallucinating. Whatever the reason, the shot was fired.

'The system came on. The chair was close to the fireplace. That would be out of view of the camera?'

'The chair, yes. The man, too, if he slumped down.'

'He wouldn't sit up very straight with a bullet through his neck. And the door?'

'Yes, the door's out of camera in most chalets.'

'So he could have fired from the door, or he could have hidden the pistol and sat down in the other chair before he fired. There'd be nothing for the porter to see but smoke, if it showed up at all. How long would he watch an empty room for?'

Mrs Heller raised her eyebrows. 'I don't pay staff to watch empty rooms, and they know it. Also, the next entry has the same timing. A noisy party in Number One. He'd accept that somebody had slammed the door, and switch straight over.'

'The porter doesn't have an indicator to show which doors are open and which are closed?'

'Why the hell should he?'

'No reason,' Keith said. 'So there we have one possible scenario, as they say on the box. He shoots. The system comes on. By luck, or because he knows to listen for the hum, he stays out of sight until it goes off again. His ex-friend is dead or dying. He lugs him outside. There are no bloodstains on the way so presumably he was dead by then. Next he – I'm back to the live one again – fetches the bowl from the kitchen and uses the chairback thing to mop up as much as he can of the blood, and chucks it into the back of the car – with the body, if that's where it is.

'Then, with some idea of confusing things and covering his tracks, he swaps the damaged chair over to his own chalet, Sixteen. But he makes one mistake. If he'd left two chairbacks in Sixteen and the missing one in Fifteen, the hole in the chair and the bloodstains might have gone unnoticed for long enough and we'd have had Hell's own job to work out when it had happened.

'All that was left to do was to shut the door and scram. That was . . . what time did you say?'

'11.48. One man alone in the white estate-car.'

'And that didn't make the porter think?'

41

'Why should it? I'm surprised that he noted it down at all. Men often arrive with one friend and leave with another. Dammit, the system's only designed as a check on customers' accounts, and on the staff doing their jobs.'

Mrs Heller's manner was beginning to show irritation, and Keith realised that, under the calm and commanding exterior, she was feeling the pressure. Anyone else he would have recommended not to get their knickers twisted, but somehow the words died unspoken. 'Of course,' he said, 'an estate-car isn't ideal for hiding a body in.'

'D-down behind the front seat with an old coat over it,' Wallace said.

'Or not,' said Mrs Heller thoughtfully. 'I think I'll have a search made of the grounds. And the roof-spaces of the two chalets.'

'Good idea,' Keith said. 'Better idea, leave it to the police. It may not all have happened just as I said, but something happened. You've got reason to believe that a serious crime was committed. You're obliged to call the fuzz.'

'Definitely no,' Mrs Heller said.

'Then I'll have to.'

'You came here in confidence,' Wallace said.

'Look, we're past that point,' Keith said. 'There's no doubt a serious crime was committed. All right, there is just the faintest possibility that the whole thing's a frame-up, but that in itself would be a crime. Anyway, a bookie would give you a thousand to one against a frame-up. Somebody got shot, and if I sit on that sort of information I could be put out of business.'

Mrs Heller sighed. 'So could we,' she said. 'We have enemies in authority who'd like fine to close us down. But we have friends as well. If we go to the fuzz with vague theories there'll be a long investigation and we're finished; but if we can go to them with a complete case and with proof that'll stand up in court, we can get it handled discreetly. We're popular with the fiscal's office. And don't look smug,' she added. 'It's not what you think. We've been able to help them a lot in the past. The girls get pillow talk. And, once, we let the police listen in when the cash from a robbery was being divvied up in one of our chalets. So if it's quick and simple we can survive. That's why I want a degree of proof that'll satisfy the law before I'll go running to it.'

Keith set his jaw stubbornly. 'I can't go along with suppression of evidence about murder by gunshot,' he said. Even to himself, his voice sounded high-pitched and querulous. 'I'm a registered dealer in firearms and my living depends on my remaining that way. So does yours,' he added to Wallace.

Mrs Heller and Wallace exchanged a long look. 'Have you explained to him?' she asked.

'Not yet.'

'I don't want to know,' Keith said. 'I've been here long enough. I've things to do. And I'm hungry. Call the police, or I will.'

Mrs Heller looked at her watch and pulled a menu out of her drawer. 'Dinner should be on now,' she said. 'Order what you like, it's on the house. Just listen a little longer.'

Keith's head was beginning to throb and a great lethargy was creeping over him, along with a continuing sense of unreality. He was about to refuse and leave, but he took a glance at the menu. It was an exceptionally good menu. The horrific prices in the margin made it more rather than less attractive. 'Pâté,' he said weakly. 'Dover sole, strawberries and cream, cheeseboard, coffee and a cigar.'

'And to drink?'

'Pint of Guinness from the pub in the village, and a Grand Marnier to follow.'

Mrs Heller suppressed a ladylike shudder. 'Certainly,' she said. She pressed the lever on her intercom and commanded that a dining table be brought in.

'I think I'll just have an omelette,' Wallace said.

'I'd better phone my wife,' Keith said. 'I think she's cooking up something special for me tonight.'

'We can give you just as good a meal as she can.'

'I didn't mean food. On second thoughts,' Keith said, 'let Wallace do the phoning. If he speaks for me, she'll know I'm not somewhere I shouldn't be.'

The pâté was real *foie gras*, the toast crisp and hot. 'All right,' Keith said with his cheek full. 'You talk, I'll listen. Then we'll decide

43

which of us calls the police.'

'I doubt it,' Wallace said. 'You'd take in what I'm going to say more easily if you'd seen the place at a weekend, or at any other time than a Tuesday afternoon at a time of year when most of the moneyed are away abroad. These girls make money. And the original objective of this place was, and still is, to protect the girls' earnings so that they can keep what they make and retire before the life kills them or some man takes it off them.'

Keith pointed his knife at Wallace. 'A Co-op. That's what you've started,' he said. 'Are you affiliated to the Movement?'

Wallace had taken the opportunity to grab a hasty bite of his omelette. He chewed quickly and swallowed. 'A Co-op, if you like. But it's a Co-op that grosses over a million a year. Any girl that doesn't pull in a hundred grand asks her best friend what she's doing wrong. About half of that stays available for reinvestment.'

'And you've been going how long?'

'Eight years, four months,' said Mrs Heller.

'Don't bother trying to do any sums,' Wallace said. 'We don't put the money in a piggy-bank, we put it to work. Mostly, we've been buying up run-down businesses and revitalising them, selling and starting again. But we'll tackle any investment that looks profitable. We've backed inventions, and several of them have paid off. And if one of the girls wants to retire as proprietor of some particular type of business – one of them wanted a grey-hound stadium, would you believe? – we buy it and let her share the running of it so that she knows what she's doing before she takes over. One of our retired ladies owns and runs the best hotel in – but I'd better not say where. I tell you, Keith, a girl can work here for three years – and that's about as long as they last – and retire rich, but *rich*.'

'I was wrong,' Keith said. 'It's not a Co-op. You've launched a bloody female Mafia on an unsuspecting world.'

'You're not far wrong,' Mrs Heller said. 'And the money side of it we owe to Wal. He has a genius for making money turn over.'

Keith just nodded. Since Wallace had joined his business, the turnover and the profits had trebled.

'Laundrettes, boutiques, even a finance house,' Wallace said. 'But the biggest of all is property. We got hooked up with a small contractor. He'd been successful in getting a housing contract but the bank wouldn't back him any more. We backed him and made a nice profit. He was a bad manager and made damn-all. So we took him over and went in for up-market speculative housing.'

Keith flushed the last of the pâté out of his mouth with a draught of the Guinness. 'With one of your girls as manager?' he asked.

'As chairperson. We've got a damn good surveyor to manage the operation. If you can find the right sites it's money for old rope. Finding sites can be a problem. But one of the new towns had a proposition. They wanted a golf course and weren't allowed the money to pay for it. So they made up a package, and we came in with the best tender. We provided the golf course, paid them a correspondingly reduced capital sum, and surrounded the golf course with top quality private housing for sale. Everybody wants to live next door to a golf course within easy commuting distance of a city. Then we sold off a package for a hotel complex and conference centre. We came out nearly a million quid ahead of the game.'

Keith started on his sole. 'None of this seems relevant,' he said, 'but I'll listen for just as long as you feed me.'

'It's relevant all right.' Wallace was lagging behind. He bolted a few mouthfuls and set off again. 'Came the day when the decision was taken to bring a pipeline ashore at Firth Bay, only a mile or two from where the rig-building yard had suddenly gained orders for a steady supply of oil platforms. Suddenly a small town was having to grow to accommodate a large number of managerial types and very highly paid workers. It also happens to be in an area with outstanding recreational possibilities, and not too inaccessible from the centres of population given some expenditure on roads.

'Trouble was, the whole thing coincided with a government squeeze on public investment.

'So we contacted the various local authorities and made a proposition, much on the lines of the new town one but expanded out of recognition. We would finance the whole package except for what grants and loans they could get from the Scottish Office. They'd get their town to a high standard, including marina, with golf courses and so on and so forth to a standard that'd attract national competitions. Of course, their piggy eyes lit up immediately, because the rating income alone will enable them to clear every slum in their combined territories and give every councillor a chauffeured Jag.

'Our profit was to come out of the private housing again, and our share of the equity of sites for the shopping centre and offices. And we were reckoning on getting that money in without too much of a time-lag.

'So we went ahead with our share of the infrastructure and started on the house-building.

'Next thing we know, the government's toughened its squeeze, there's what amounts to a ban on mortgages, the pipeline's hit a technical snag and the whole project's gone slow because of political and contractual in-fighting.

'We'd already made a start to building our houses. Now we had to make a decision. Stopping could be damned expensive – unfinished work and unbuilt materials rotting or being vandalised, workforce scattered, subcontracts lapsing with entitlement to compensation and so on. On the other hand, at a time of roaring inflation it could be a good investment to keep on building. The houses'd be worth half as much again by the time we sold them. The extra cost of a few watchmen was trifling.

'The snag, of course, was the drain on capital. We pledged everything that we could, and it wasn't going to be enough. So we decided to go public.'

Keith dropped his knife and fork, and his voice went squeaky with horror. 'Wal,' he said, 'not even you could get away with offering shares on the Stock Exchange in a brothel.'

'We're not offering shares in any such thing,' Wallace said patiently. 'We're offering shares in a sound and substantial group of companies. No company in the world can afford to be fussy about the possible origins of all its capital. I dare say that some of the investors will be the real Mafia.'

'The male one,' said Mrs Heller. 'The point is that shares go on the market in three weeks time. If anything rocks the boat we have a financial disaster on our hands.'

Keith finished his sole and sighed. It had been delicious. 'The sudden revelation that the headquarters and foundation of the

46

group of companies was a knocking-shop would rock the boat all right,' Keith said. 'And a murder thrown in for good measure wouldn't help a lot. But it's your financial disaster. My heart bleeds for all the young ladies who'll lose their dowries, but you've shown me no good reason why I should get my neck in a sling with the fuzz by compounding a felony.'

'Then,' Wallace said, 'here it comes. We're making a good living out of the business, you and I, but nothing like enough to support the investment in what you call stock and what we both know is your private collection of ancient armaments at several thousand quid each.'

'Only for the best pieces,' Keith said. 'And you know it's money well invested.'

'Considering the rate that you borrowed it at, yes. You may recall that I negotiated very favourable loans for you, even considering the low rate then prevailing, both for the business and for your loan on Briesland House, repayment period unspecified.'

The first strawberries turned to dust and ashes in Keith's mouth. 'That wasn't –?'

'That was our finance house,' Mrs Heller said. 'We agreed to it as a favour to Wal. The finance house is backing the development business. If the shit hits the fan, we'll let those two go to the wall and save the rest.'

'The liquidator,' Wallace said, 'will undoubtedly call in all out-standing loans. You'll have to sell your whole collection or borrow again, and the present interest rate is an all-time high.'

Keith did a few sums in his head and disliked the answers intensely. He glared at his partner.'You're the *capo* of a female Mafia,' he said, 'and I don't believe this is really happening.'

Wallace helped himself to biscuits and Cheddar. He always favoured the harder cheeses although his missing fingers made the holding of a cheese-knife difficult. 'You'd better believe it,' he said. 'Only I'm not the *capo*, Debbie is. I'm only their financial adviser. And yours. And I'm advising you very strongly to play along.'

Debbie Heller smiled angelically. 'I'm told that you're quite an investigator where guns and shooting are concerned. If you help us out by investigating this ... this suspected crime, and

47

we can thereby save our bacon, you can forget your loans and we'll pay for your time on top, plus a bonus.'

There was a lengthening silence. Keith popped another strawberry into his mouth. It tasted much better. He washed it down with the last of his Guinness. Marvellous. 'I wouldn't expect to work for a lesser hourly rate than one of your girls would charge me,' he said.

Wallace whistled, but Mrs Heller only raised her charming eyebrows. 'Of course not,' she said. 'Why should you, as long as you put the same dedication into it?'

'You may not like what I uncover.'

'And I may love it. You may find two old friends walking around, one of them with his arm in a sling.'

'What,' Keith asked, 'would you consider a reasonable bonus if I did save your bacon?'

'What would you?'

'The Ferguson rifle out of that chalet.'

Wallace choked on his coffee. 'Now just a holy minute,' he said.

'Let him have it,' Mrs Heller said. 'It's just an old gun.'

'It's a bloody valuable old gun,' Wallace said. 'It's a piece of history and a collector's dream. There were only about a hundred made, and they went out to America during the War of Independence. God alone knows what happened to most of the rest of them but there's one in a museum in New Jersey. Keith, I told you what we paid for those guns. Without the Ferguson, would you pay us our money back for the rest of them?'

Keith crossed his fingers under the table. 'Certainly,' he said.

'Well all right. But, Debbie, I've a feeling you're being conned.'

'If we are,' Mrs Heller said, 'you share in the profits. And it's worth it if we can only find out. So don't get your balls in an uproar.'

Keith attacked the cheese and biscuits with enthusiasm. Of recent years he had come to appreciate a good meal. He never put on an ounce of weight. Molly, however, had put on a pound or two since the baby was born, and when Molly went on a diet *everybody* did the same. 'Of course,' he said, 'I can't guarantee that you'll like the answer.'

'Just get me the answer and leave the bacon-saving to me.'

When the table had been removed, Keith took a pull at his cigar and burped politely. 'All right,' he said. 'So I don't go running to Chief Inspector Munro. You believe that the whole thing might be a frame-up, or a relatively harmless mishap. Why not let the sleeping dog lie?'

Mrs Heller shook her head vehemently. The glasses slid down her nose and she pushed them back with an impatient finger. 'Bugger that,' she said. The words sounded almost ladylike on her lips. 'I want to *know*. There may be a wave of events about to break over us. And if there's been a murder done . . .'

'What, then?' Keith asked.

'Then I'll have a bloody difficult decision to make.'

Keith looked at her. She meant it. 'We've got two lines of enquiry,' he said. 'The first starts inside here. We need a detailed examination of who did what, where and when. We need everything anyone can remember. We need a list of all the times and events in your log-book and so on. And we need a detailed examination of the chalets, waste-bins, contents of vacuum cleaners, what's missing, that sort of thing.'

'I'll see to that,' Mrs Heller said. 'I'm not having outsiders trampling around, barging in on couples and frightening the clients. You'll get everything gathered up for you. And I'll get all that she can remember out of Annette as soon as she gets back.'

'Is she included in your security clamp-down, or could she be saying the wrong thing?'

'I spoke to her on the phone. I didn't tell her anything or ask any questions, but I put the shits up her. She'll do a lot of listening and damn-all talking until she gets back. What else?'

'Start your staff looking round the grounds. Work outwards from Number Fifteen. Look for recently disturbed earth.' As he finished speaking Keith fell silent, his eyes fixed on a corner of the ceiling.

Mrs Heller opened her mouth, but Wallace gestured for silence. Keith blinked and looked around. 'He was thinking,' Wallace said.

'Is that what it was? I thought he just died.'

'You can't hide much in an estate-car,' Keith said. 'And I don't just mean bodies. If you don't take everything out of it every

49

night it turns into a junk-pile and every thief can see what you've got. Especially, you don't leave shooting gear on show, because you might lead a thief home to your guns.

'Whoever it was, the shooter or the shootee, obviously didn't have a pistol in the car or yours wouldn't have been borrowed. Unless mucking up your pistol was a deliberate act intended to deceive, which doesn't seem to have much point. But he did have some gunpowder, and at least one ball and a percussion cap. That suggests that he had his bag or box of gear with him.

'If he was a pistol enthusiast, he'd have had a smaller cap than a military top hat with him. He could be a clay pigeon man, using a smoothbore musket as a shotgun and occasionally firing a ball at targets. We've no way of knowing whether he had a musket or a shotgun with him. If he wanted to sneak up on the other man, he couldn't have hidden a five-foot musket down his trouser-leg; so he borrowed a pistol.

'If he had the rest of his gear with him, the odds are that he had his long-arm with him as well, be it musket or shotgun, because if you take one out of the car you take both.

'This is pretty much of a long shot, because he may have been on his way to shoot deer or something. But suppose he had the whole gubbins in his car because he was going to or coming back from some competition.'

'Like where?'

'That's the question. And the reason the answer's highly speculative is because there may be small, local competitions I don't know about. But Bisley was a month ago, and there's nothing on for the next fortnight that I can think of unless you count a branch meeting in west Wales.

'Except for the Game Fair. It's in Yorkshire this year, not so very far away. Every shooting man who can get away makes the pilgrimage. There's always a lot of clay-shooting at a Game Fair, and this year the *Shooting Times* trophy for muzzle-loaders is being shot for as well. Any shooting man with an interest in antique guns will be there. Our man may have been intending to fetch up there.'

'When is it?' Mrs Heller asked.

'Three days, starting the day after tomorrow.'

'But Keith,' Wallace said plaintively, 'even if you were right, would he still go?'

'He would if he's been telling his pals he'd be there. It'd be more risky to stay away and make people think. Is there any more coffee?'

Mrs Heller poured coffee. 'As you said, it's one hell of a long shot. But unless the staff here come up with something, we just have no lead at all to the identities of the men. It's worth a go.'

'That's what I thought,' Keith said. 'I was hoping to sneak down for a day. But now I think we might make a three-day jaunt of it. Could we borrow Miss Hilary.'

'No you could not,' Mrs Heller snapped. 'For one thing, she has appointments and we don't break appointments lightly around here. For another, I'm not having her put in danger.'

'Danger?'

'Yes, danger. Do think about it. Suppose you're right. Suppose some man did a killing here, with that pistol. There's nothing to connect him at the moment except that he goes in for these old guns and that Hilary knows his face. He's fool enough to go and shoot. He's there with his gun in his hands and he sees the one person who could identify him. What would his reaction be?'

'We could disguise her in a wig and dark glasses. And clothes.'

'Could you disguise her voice? Or her walk?'

Keith thought about Miss Hilary's walk. He thought that given a few hours alone with her he could have her walking bow-legged, but he kept silent.

'Keith,' said Wallace, 'what would Molly's reaction be if you took Hilary to the Game Fair with you?'

'*You* could take her,' Keith said.

Wallace curled his lip and did not bother to answer.

'Now listen to me,' Mrs Heller said. Both men listened. 'You've no way of knowing that only those two men were involved. It could just as easily be that the man in Sixteen went for a walk, and some enemy of the man in Fifteen took the opportunity to blow him away. And there's no one person around here that would know the face of every customer.'

'That's a problem. You could hardly declare a holiday and bring half-a-dozen of them along to the Game Fair.'

Mrs Heller smiled grimly. 'We're not *that* game,' she said. 'If you're envisaging a caravan-bordello on Italian wartime lines, put it out of your pointed head.'

Wallace leaned forward suddenly. 'How about a photographer? Or more than one? B-bring back a record of everybody who shoots a muzzle-loader, or even pauses to look on.'

'Excellent,' said Mrs Heller.

'But,' Keith said, 'where do we pick up a photographer at short notice, available for three days?'

'Molly,' Wallace said. 'She's very good with a camera,' he explained to Debbie Heller. 'Illustrates books and things.'

'We're not involving my wife in this.'

'We're not involving her,' Wallace pointed out, 'and she doesn't have to come out here. We tell her that somebody's trying to track down a man who bought a flintlock on the never-never and defaulted, or something like that. She can stay back at a distance and use one of those wildlife lenses of hers. She could even earn herself something new and fancy in photographic gear. She wouldn't be in any danger, people are always snapping away for magazines and so on.'

'I suppose so,' Keith said.

'We could shut the shop and all go down. Take my Land Rover and borrow Hamish's caravan.'

Keith thought about it, and the more he thought the more he liked the idea. Mid-summer was the slackest season in the shop. Even fishing-tackle was hardly paying the rates. And he enjoyed game fairs. 'We could try and get a share of somebody's stand. I'll start some telephoning in a minute.'

'First, one more thing.' He produced the lead ball. 'Could you get a sample of this analysed?'

Mrs Heller nodded. 'Of course,' she said. 'But what for?'

'I want to know the percentage contents of antimony, cadmium and silver.'

'Silver?' Wallace said. Witchcraft came into his mind.

'Yes. We've been assuming a muzzle-loading enthusiast, probably with a replica gun and using a mould to make his own lead balls. But he might be an antiques man, either a dealer or a collector. He might have had a cased original with him, in which

52

case the ball would probably be original too. Or Wallace could have made a mistake; maybe our man found a pistol still loaded with the original ball.'

'I didn't,' Wallace said.

'It's worth checking. Early lead had a silver content, because they didn't have any process for extracting it.

'And now,' Keith said, 'lend me your telephone and I'll see whether we can't get a share of stand-space at the Game Fair.' It was not in his nature to do one thing at a time if he could do ten, especially if he could show a profit on each of them.

Four

Keith had a loose working arrangement with several other importers and stockists of muzzle-loading guns and equipment, aimed at avoiding unnecessary duplication of items which might be sold only once in a blue moon. Among these was the Nottinghamshire firm of P. Holdbright, and by happy chance Paddy Holdbright had a stand at the Game Fair. Even more happily, he had inadvertently taken more space than he needed, and was delighted to get rid of half the space in exchange of two-thirds of the cost.

Suddenly, Keith's little world was in turmoil.

Molly incautiously agreed to undertake an unspecified photographic task in exchange for an enormous zoom lens which she had long coveted and which, she said happily, could bring up the hairs on a flea's leg at fifty yards in the dark. ('At that price,' Wallace said sourly, 'it would need to.')

Stock, baby-gear and household necessities were crammed any-old-how into the caravan, and none too early on the Wednesday morning the two men, their wives and dogs and the baby were in the Land Rover and on the road south. By late that night they were installed in the caravan park at Upperleigh Abbey, the stock was in the tent where Paddy Holdbright would sleep on guard over his own stock at night, and some sort of order prevailed.

It would be untrue to suggest that the fair was uneventful until the Saturday morning.

The expected crowds duly arrived, thinly on the Thursday, building up through Friday and on the Saturday into a deluge. The weather, in Game Fair tradition, was scorching.

Money was burning a hole in many a pocket. People had come to watch the dog-trials and the fly-casting contests, to study game-rearing, to shop for guns, gear or books, to see the falconry, to swap ferrets on the pugs-and-drummers stand, to ask questions along Gunmaker's Row, to enjoy, to participate, to learn. The bars did boom business.

The route between the car parks and the fair led past the clay pigeon layout, and for once the muzzle-loaders were conspicuously placed. Interest caught, and the few stands covering the subject were in a state of siege. Keith had been told that he was mad to bring so much stock, but he began to worry about running out. He began booking orders instead of making cash sales.

Keith took an hour off on the Friday, and ran the dogs in a gundog test. The spaniel was feeling her age and ran badly. But the young Labrador was placed.

At about eleven on the Saturday morning Molly, complete with baby and pram, appeared outside the stand. She began making anguished faces at Keith. Recognising the symptoms, Keith concluded his sales-talk to a customer with unaccustomed haste, slapping some brochures into the man's hand and almost gabbling, 'For this you need a firearms certificate, you can have *this* on a shotgun certificate, that one's only a wall-hanger, and this kit doesn't need any certificates until you drill out the vent. Let me know what you decide.' He was gone before the man had finished nodding.

He joined Molly beyond the small throng that was pricing his rack of powder-horns. Wallace darted out from behind the counter. 'Is Janet all right?' Wallace asked.

Molly nodded breathlessly.

'What's up, then?'

'Somebody pinched my bag of films ... now don't get het up,' she said quickly. She paused for a few deep breaths. Her pretty face was flushed and her dark hair tousled. Keith thought that she must have brought the pram up from the shooting-ground like a dragster. 'He only got the unused films,' she went on. 'I was dropping the exposed ones into my pocket, but from a distance it could have looked as if I was putting them into the bag. I was using one of your old fishing-bags, Keith. It was at my feet, but when I looked down it was gone.'

'It could have been a casual thief,' Keith said. 'Is Janet still covering the place?'

'Yes. The film in the camera will last an hour or so, because I told Janet just to take each group.'

Wallace showed sign of imminent panic. 'Janet should have a bodyguard,' he said. 'If he realises that he only got unused film ...'

'Want to go?'

'Yes. No. I want to get this film away for processing. But I want Janet under guard.'

'Right,' Keith said. 'I'll go and stand guard. No point looking for an old fishing-bag in this crowd. Molly can stay here and mind the shop and the baby, you do the doings and then come back here and relieve Molly. Yes?'

'Yes.'

'You can buy film at the end of the next row,' Molly said. 'Janet knows how to reload.'

Keith disappeared. Molly emptied the cassettes of exposed film out of her pockets into a carrier-bag and Wallace grabbed it. Molly hung on. 'There were two lenses and a meter in that bag,' she said.

'We'll replace them.'

Molly let go. Wallace plunged way. Molly sighed. She manoeuvred the pram into the back of the tent and turned to face the counter. A prosperous-looking customer buttonholed her on the subject of a reproduction percussion shotgun.

'You can have it against a shotgun certificate,' Molly said. It was an oft-repeated refrain. 'But if you want black powder for it you'll need a Form F from the police. Including V.A.T., the price –'

Keith reappeared beside her. He had a powder-horn and a shot-pouch slung over his shoulder. He took the gun firmly out of her hands. 'It's out of stock for the next hour,' he said. 'If I've got to hang around down at the clay pigeons, I may as well get some shooting in.'

'I was going to buy it,' the man said plaintively.

'Buy it later,' Molly said. 'He's the boss.'

The man turned to Keith. 'Double or quits you can't beat fourteen out of twenty.'

'You're on,' Keith said.

They went away together. Molly started showing cleaning kits to the next in line.

Monday morning saw all four at work in the shop, back in

56

Newton Lauder. While Molly attended to the sporadic trickle of customers and Janet, grumbling, restored order to the stock which had come back from the Game Fair, Keith and Wallace sat in the cluttered back-shop, balancing up the books.

The trip had been profitable. 'But,' Wallace said, 'there's a hundred and sixty quid here that I can't account for.'

'That's mine,' Keith said. 'It's the bet I won.'

'So it is.' Wallace looked at him sideways. 'But your bet doubled the sale price of an item of stock. The profit belongs to the business. I hope that you're not thinking of charging Debbie Heller your full rate for a trip that you made a bomb out of anyway.'

'*We* made the bomb. You're part of this business too, you know. You may be financial whizz-kid to a superior knocking-shop –'

Wallace drew himself up. 'I am not –' he began hotly.

'Would they have underwritten us if we'd made a loss?'

'Probably. But we'd have had to try bloody hard to make a loss with you charging your hourly rate.'

'Whose side are you on?' Keith demanded.

'It's not a question of sides. It's a matter of common honesty.'

'You keep telling me they're loaded.'

Wallace lowered his voice. 'This may come as a surprise to you, but they didn't make it just to give it to you.' The success of his argument over Keith's winnings made him incautious. 'Those girls work bloody hard. They don't just lie around all day.'

Keith lit up in an enormous grin. 'No? What alternative positions –'

The argument, though *sotto voce*, was in full flood when the telephone rang. Wallace lifted it and listened. 'We'll be right over,' he said, and disconnected. 'Debbie Heller wants to see us right away. It sounded urgent.'

'Madam calls, so we go?'

'When that kind of money calls, everybody goes,' Wallace said.

They made feeble excuses to their disenchanted wives.

Five

Their return to Millmont House seemed to coincide with the departure of late stragglers from Sunday night's business. At the gate they met a vast American car with darkened windows and a dusky chauffeur, and in the drive they passed a crimson Jaguar with a driver whose dark glasses and pulled-down hat failed to hide the symptoms of nervous exhaustion.

The house itself seemed a haven of calm respectability. Keith parked under the tree opposite the front door. 'If they crap on it, they crap on it,' he said. An unfamiliar porter showed them into Mrs Heller's office.

The lady nodded them into chairs and then paused. Keith was struck afresh by the contrast she presented. In appearance she was a beautiful woman, sometimes slightly past her best, sometimes as now, with her thick-rimmed glasses sliding down her nose, a child. But always there lay behind her calm front a spectrum of personalities – calculating, sometimes ribald, stern, compassionate and ethical. Even moral, if the word were not so inapposite. Keith understood women, but he wondered whether he would ever understand this one.

'First,' she said, 'I think I'd better tell you about our visitor. We may have had more than one. Anybody – any man – can ring us up, make an appointment, come, look us over and go. But there's one that we're sure of. He phoned at about the time you left on Tuesday, asked for and got an appointment with Hilary, and came on Wednesday. He made sure that he got his money's worth first. Then he started asking her questions about her Sunday evening visitor and his friend. Had they seemed on good terms? Did they leave together? Was anything unusual said? Was any hint given as to where they were going next? That sort of thing.

'She told him nothing – or so she says – and when he left she called up Charlie who was on the desk. So we caught him when he came to pay the bill.'

Keith's eyebrows shot up. 'Even with a first-timer, you don't take payment in advance?'

'We prefer not to. He may order drinks or go over his time.' Mrs Heller seemed amused. 'We don't get gypped more than once a year, if that. Nobody can get a car out of the gate if we don't want them to. One man did come in in a stolen car once, and climbed the gate going out. Then he tried it again a year later. We made him wash up in the kitchen for a fortnight.

'Charlie brought him in here.' She pushed her hair back with a tired gesture. 'I can't say that either of us got much out of it. Each of us wanted to find out as much as possible without saying a damn thing. I couldn't push it too hard without giving away that I was anxious. I made out the we're always suspicious when somebody makes inquiries, and he cracked on that he was trying to find a missing friend. In the end we both gave up and he pissed off. He was a big man, over six feet and about fifteen stone, a bit of a belly but muscular with it. Age about forty, maybe a little less. Brown hair going grey at the temples, and a very ordinary sort of face. He booked in as Jonathan Brown.

'The same night, Charlie came back from the village pub. Another man had tried to pump him. This one was smaller, grey-haired, with a thin face and a big, curved nose. Charlie said that he was a snazzy dresser, but the bigger man was a scruff.

'With so much interest being taken in us, I thought I'd better bring forward the annual check. I called in the man who designed and installed our electronic systems.'

'Jake Paterson?'

She looked at Keith sharply. 'He talked?'

'Not a word. He's a neighbour of mine, and it has his sort of ingenuity written all over it.'

'I see. Well, he came and checked the place over with another gadget. He found transmitter bugs in here, under the desk and also under your chair. He'll have had some funny listening off that one. So it looks as if he came prepared to be fetched in here. And there was another transmitter attached to our T.V. circuits, outdoors. We're clean again now. I don't think he could have learned anything useful, and if he wants his equipment back he'll have to dig under the new swimming-pool for it.'

'A pity,' Keith said. 'We could have used it to mislead.'

'I thought of it, but we don't know enough. Almost anything that we said could turn out true. We never found out where the receivers were, but a grey car was parked up on the hill for a couple of days. It's gone now.'

'I suppose nobody got the number?'

'It was gone before we knew it was there. Anyway, your pal Paterson said that the equipment was good-quality, German stuff of standard makes. He said it was the kind of gear an agency might use, official or private. He's checking us over twice a week until this is all over, and no strangers get to come in here any more.'

'Next thing.' She took a fat envelope out of a drawer. 'I've got your photographs.'

'Now, how the hell,' Keith asked, 'would you get them done so quickly over a weekend?'

'I whistled up the taxi-plane,' Wallace said.

Mrs Heller smiled gently. 'We have a professional photographer for a client. He's more interested in the photographs he can get of himself with a time-lapse camera than in what he's doing. I think they turn him on his wife. Well, she's due for a surprise. For a little extra co-operation he worked all day yesterday.' She slid a small selection of photographs, clipped together, out of the envelope. 'We've passed them round all the girls and the porters. Four of our clients appear in the photographs, but only one was here that night or for a month before that. Hilary's customer.'

She slid the photographs across the desk and Keith and Wallace studied them together. There were three prints in all. The first showed a group of men waiting to shoot. Two of them were in the act of loading, and one of these was ringed. The second print showed the same man raising his gun to fire, while the third was a blow-up of part of the same photograph, concentrating on his head and the hands holding the gun.

The man was lean and dark and he looked intense. He must have been insufferably hot in his shooting-jacket, but Keith guessed that he wore it for the many pockets that held wads and cards and pricker and percussion caps. In the group photograph, he seemed to be of average height or less, and he was probably the lightest man in the group.

60

'Don Donaldson,' Mrs Heller said.

Wallace grunted. 'Not a customer that I've seen in the shop.'

'We might show Molly the photograph,' Keith said. 'He may have recognised her, even if she didn't recognise him at the time.' He took the blow-up out of Wallace's hand. The detail was sharp. 'That's a Kentucky rifle. Very odd!'

'Would it take the ball that we dug out of the chair?' Mrs Heller asked.

'Don't rush me. Let me think aloud. That ball would have fitted some Kentucky rifles – Pennsylvania long rifle, to give it its proper name. But this isn't an antique, it's a reproduction. The ones I know are smaller calibre. But he wouldn't be trying for clay pigeons with a rifled barrel. Wal, what did I say the ball weighed?'

'Near as dammit three-quarters of an ounce. Your very words.'

'What's that times twenty?'

'Fifteen ounces,' Wallace said promptly.

'Just under a pound. In other words, the ball would go up a twenty-bore barrel with room to spare for a patch.' Keith looked at Mrs Heller and smiled. 'Never mind my havering. The point is that there's a twenty-bore shotgun version of this rifle, which could take the ball. What's more, this had been built from a kit. The brass patch-box hasn't been inletted well, and the line of the comb looks wrong. Wal, who was it made a twenty-bore Kentucky kit?'

'Pedersoli, I think. We never stocked it, though.'

'No. It isn't even in the current catalogues. It was for the American market. Paddy imported a few, but they didn't go well and he gave them up. Shall I speak to him?'

Mrs Heller put her hand on the telephone. 'Number?'

Keith pulled out his diary. The back pages were crammed with addresses and phone-numbers. Mrs Heller relayed the number to the porter on the desk. 'One other thing,' she said to Keith. She handed him a letter. 'The analysis of the lead ball.'

Keith took the headed paper and glanced quickly down the lines of typing. 'One and a half percent antimony,' he said, 'no tin, no calcium, no silver.'

'Not antique, then,' Mrs Heller said.

61

'Not ordinary scrap lead either,' said Wallace.

'I think,' Keith said, 'that he must have been casting lead balls out of spent bullets. Which might make him a member of a rifle club. But then again, he might have got permission to clean out the target area of a club or a territorial army range or something.'

Mrs Heller's telephone made a servile noise. She picked it up, listened for a second and then handed it to Keith. 'Mr Holdbright's on the line.'

Keith took the phone. For a minute he exchanged friendly insults and compared notes about the Game Fair with Paddy, and then he got down to business. 'Paddy, I'm trying to get in touch with somebody who did me a favour at the Game Fair. He was shooting a twenty-bore version of the Pennsylvania long rifle, built from a kit. I think you were the only importer..? Could you put me in touch with him?'

The receiver made miniature mutterings for several minutes. Keith gave Paddy the phone-number of Millmont House. 'Thanks,' he said. 'I'll do the same for you some day.' He disconnected. 'If I don't see you coming. He only sold four of those kits. One went abroad. It may have come back, of course, but he doesn't think so. Two went to customers he knows well. One of those isn't finished, because Paddy's got it back to bore the ramrod pipe. The other definitely wasn't at the Game Fair, and anyway the man's Form F isn't through yet. The fourth was sold by post, somewhere up this way he thinks. He's looking up the name and address and he'll call me back.'

'While we're waiting,' Wallace said. 'J-just a thought. If those two visitors, the ones who bugged the place, are from an agency, somebody in the credit business might know them.'

'Good thought,' said Debbie Heller.

'And I know people in the credit business,' Wallace finished up.

'So you do. But I know somebody who spends half his time having credit checked.' She pressed down a lever on her intercom. 'Gordon, dear ...'

While she spoke to her husband, Keith was amused to see yet another facet of Debbie Heller appear. She adored her husband. Although in effect she was handing out orders, she spoke in a lover's tones. There was a faint blush on her cheek, and she twined her legs together. A startling weakness, Keith thought, in a tiger-minded ex-tart.

'He'll see what he can find out from the agencies we use,' she said when the call was finished. 'Now . . .' she took some papers out of a folder on her desk. 'While you were making money and enjoying yourselves down at the Game Fair, I was –'

'Making money and enjoying yourself up here,' Keith said.

She gave him a look that almost gave him hypothermia. 'I was unremuneratively and miserably interviewing every member of this establishment, without getting any further forward. It seems that Don Donaldson had that part of the grounds to himself on Sunday night. My staff are consistent in their stories, bear each other out and are corroborated in every respect by the records. I've had a search made of both chalets and the ground between and around, and if there's anything significant to be learned I'll – I'll submit to rape by a mad donkey. We've saved you lots of little bags of Hoover contents, rubbish from waste baskets and pedal bins, and path-sweepings. And the best of British luck with them!

'Last of all, while you were down at the Game Fair making money and having fun,' she said firmly, 'I was wading through all the records, the chits, accounts, computerised bookings and the log, and I've listed everything that relates to those two girls or the two chalets and which could possibly be relevant.' She gave Keith and Wallace each a page of neatly typed notes. 'None of it takes us much further, but it's a framework to hang more facts on as we get them.'

Keith began to read the notes. Each was preceded by a number, eight digits from the computer, four if the entry was from the porters' log.

(Wednesday)
1935 Booking. Fosdyke for self (no pref) and Donaldson (Hilary). Saturday nogo. Booked Sunday 1900. Dinner – trs to Catering.
(Sunday)
1410 Gate. Visitor, Hilary, 16. H notified.
1456 Dr, visitor ex 16.
1705 Annette. Needs extra chalet at 1900. Booked 15.
1835 Dr, Hilary into 15.

1846 Dr, Annette + visitor exq.

1854 Gate. Visitors for 15. Wh Granada Est.

1915 Dinner to 15. (The meal was printed in detail. Keith whistled respectfully. The men had done themselves well).

2134 Warning call, Hilary.

2139 Dr, Annette ex 15.

2143 Dr, Annette into 9.

2153 Gate. Visitor, Hilary, re M.G. Spoke 16, still visitor. Booked 4. Dr, Hilary ex 16.

2205 Dr, Hilary's visitor into 4.

2221 *No 15 Man. Says let door slam.

'If he let the door slam,' Keith said, 'he was inside to speak to the porter. How did he get out? That has to be the shot.'

An incoming telephone call interrupted him. Paddy Holdbright. Keith listened, expressed gratitude and put the phone down. 'It was posted out to a Mr. J. M. Scott in Perth,' he said. 'Would your porter find out whether he's on the phone?'

'Of course,' Mrs Heller said. She gave a crisp instruction, without explanation, over the intercom. She blinked at Keith from behind her glasses. 'But would anybody describe Perth as 'Somewhere up this way?'

'Paddy would,' Wallace said. 'I don't think he's been north of Newcastle in his life. If the address said Scotland . . .'

Keith had gone back to the notes.

2236 Dr. Hilary into 4.

2344 A/C for 15 settled, cash.

2348/Gate. White Granada Est out, driver only.

Dr. Visitor ex 4.

(Monday)

1022 Dr. Hilary ex 4.

1345 Dr. Hilary into 16.

1412 *No 16. Hilary says damaged chair.

He was still looking at the list, trying to extract some meaning from it and wondering what was missing, when the porter's voice came over the intercom to say that there was no telephone in Perth listed to a J. M. Scott at the address given by Paddy Holdbright. One was listed for a different address. He had spoken to the man's wife, who was positive that they had not moved

64

house in fifteen years. She had shrieked with laughter at the suggestion that her husband might be competent to build a gun from a kit.

Mr Heller followed the porter on the intercom. He had a pleasant voice, accentless. Keith noticed a nice balance between affection and respect, and developed his own suspicions as to who wore the black lace trousers in that household. 'They don't work for any Edinburgh agency,' Mr Heller was saying. 'I phoned the J.D.V. Agency in Glasgow – they *only* do credit-checking, so I could be sure that the men weren't theirs. They checked with a contact who does divorces, and called me back. They came up with two names. The big one that you know as Jonathan Brown could be Jim Bardolph – note the coincidence of initials? The other man sounds to them like a Cyril Warrender who works with Bardolph. The two have done some free-lancing, some of it verging on industrial espionage. They have a bad reputation. But lately they've been working for the Granton and Green agency in Motherwell. That's all I could find out.'

'Thank you. You've done very well.' The words were a pat on the head for a good dog. She clicked off the intercom and pressed down another lever. The porter answered. 'Get me the Granton and Green agency in Motherwell,' she said. 'They'll be listed under Private Enquiries, or some such.'

'What are you going to say?' Wallace asked.

'I don't know. Play it off the cuff. Bluff a little and see what I can get.'

A few seconds later, the Granton and Green agency was on the line. 'I want to speak to the person in charge,' she said. 'This is the chairperson of the Personal Service group of companies. Yes, I'll hold on for Mr Green for thirty seconds. After that I go elsewhere.'

There was a pause of not more than ten seconds.

'Mr Green? This is Mrs Heller. I'm speaking from Millmont House. You sent two operators through to bug my room and the C.C.T.V. system. You needn't bother denying it, the men were James Bardolph and Cyril Warrender. You'd better believe it! Yes, boy, will I be making trouble! Unless I get a little cooperation. Bugging's illegal, I'll have you know.' She listened for a full minute, and when she spoke again her voice sounded amused but her eyes were hard. 'My dear man, I suggest that you read up your law. Our chalets are owned individually by the girls and I can show you the conveyances. We do not advertise, solicit or cause a nuisance. We've stood up to the procurator fiscal before and no doubt we'll do it again. I can make a damned sight more trouble for you than you can for me. So take my advice. I want the name of your client, and I'm prepared to pay you a thou' for it. Otherwise I rock your little boat and the hell with you! Twenty?' Her voice was outraged. 'You're out of your skull. I'll go to two thou' and that's my top figure. Take it or I'll find your client on my own, and I'll tell him that you gave me his name for twenty quid and a free ride on one of the girls.'

Mrs Heller listened in silence to the squawking of the receiver for a few seconds. Then she switched on her telephone amplifier. The man's voice came through, clear but metallic, with a Glasgow-Irish accent that could have done duty as an anvil. Keith could hear the strain of rapid thought in his brief hesitations. 'An area of common interest,' he was saying. 'My client thinks something happened at your place, a week past Sunday. If it didn't, you wouldn't want to know who he is. My guess is we're both trying to find out the same things. Now, I don't know what he's really after, but I know that nobody's after you. We've got the choice of working together and sorting it all out, or working against each other and maybe laying an egg. Either way, you don't need the name of my client.'

'I want to have it all the same.'

'Confidentiality's part of my stock-in-trade.'

'Stock-in-trade is for selling,' Mrs Heller pointed out. 'And I've been taping this call.' She winked at Wallace.

'So have I. And that means you can't edit it.' The distant Mr Green seemed to have been through similar permutations before. 'And I've got your threat on tape, so don't come that one.'

There was a silence. 'I want to think it over,' Mrs Heller said at last, calmly.

'So do I. Send somebody over to trade information and we'll see. Otherwise you know my figure.'

'At twenty thou' you can get stuffed.'

66

'You too, hen, likely for much less. And I mean that sincerely.'
They heard him hang up.

In a thoughtful tone of voice Mrs Heller suggested that Mr Green was not only illegitimate but addicted to a startling range of perversions. Her imagery was not mere vulgarity. At one point Keith found himself with a clear and hilarious mental picture of a dwarf Mr Green performing an illegal act with a reluctant penguin.

'He probably wasn't taping, any more than I was,' she finished.

'I wouldn't take any chance on it,' Wallace said.

'I'm not going to. Would you like some lunch.'

Keith would have enjoyed another free meal of Millmont House standard, but Wallace said quickly that they'd better be getting back to the business and Keith could hardly deny it.

'Very well,' Debbie Heller said. She looked at Keith. 'You'll follow up Mr Scott of Perth and see where he leads. Then, if we still don't know who Mr Green's client is you could go and see him and find out what you can. There's no point paying out good money to buy information we could get another way.'

Keith was no more chauvinistic than any other male, but taking orders from a woman offended against his vague belief that man should be the dominant partner. 'You leave it to me,' he said. 'I'll do whatever's best.'

Mrs Heller smiled sweetly. 'All right,' she said. 'You do that. Now tell me please, what's the best that you're going to do?'

Keith smiled back while he thought furiously. 'I think I'll go and see Mr Scott of Perth,' he said at last.

'Good idea,' she said. 'I'm glad you thought of that.'

Wallace gave one of his rare laughs.

As they were leaving, Keith paused in the doorway. 'You know,' he said, 'too many of us promote ourselves out of what we do really well. A woman as beautiful as you are is wasted in management.'

She smiled again, but brilliantly this time, and touched her hair. After the door had closed two vertical lines appeared between her eyebrows and the smile became uncertain. It was as if a mist had come over the sun.

Keith looked at the guano which was spattered over his car.

'She was right,' he said.

'She usually is,' Wallace said. 'Especially about the shitty side of life.'

Six

Keith dropped Wallace at the shop and took Molly back to Briesland House for lunch. Molly spooned carefully-sieved guck into the baby while Keith made a snack. The baby fell comfortably asleep. Keith and Molly sat down together.

'I've got to go up to Perth tomorrow for Wal's client,' Keith said. 'You want to come? The snag is that I don't know how long it'll take. I may have to stay over, or even go on somewhere else. You could leave Thingy with Janet, or bring her along.'

'Deborah. Not Thingy.'

'Deborah, then.'

Molly considered, nibbling away at her corn-on-the-cob, butter running down her chin. When she had first met Keith, he had been itinerant in his life and in his spirit, a wandering lover with more mistresses than she cared to think about. He was still a happy sensualist, loving her but revering the whole feminine gender. Since their marriage his comparative fidelity had assuaged her deep concern. As far as she could tell his lapses had been unplanned, no more than sudden failures to resist temptation and of no long-term importance. Molly could suffer them if she could keep Keith's heart. One reason for her success as Keith's wife was that she had avoided showing jealousy. The other was that she rarely sent him away on his own, and never with his passion unsatisfied.

'This client,' she said. 'It's Personal Service, isn't it? I've heard Wallace mention them.'

'That's right,' Keith said. He waited for the storm to break. He was accustomed to getting away with more than most husbands would have dreamed of, but not even Molly would tolerate a business relationship with a house of ill-fame.

Molly nodded, satisfied. If Wallace had brought Keith into it then it must be perfectly respectable. 'I looked them up in the phone book. They're big. They've got lots of businesses. Did you know that they do our laundry? They've got several antique shops and a finance house. They could be very useful to you. If you're doing business for them you'd better take plenty of clean shirts and things. I won't come. It wouldn't be fair on Thingy.'

'Deborah,' Keith said. 'I'll need the car. Shall I take you in to the shops this afternoon?'

'I'll drive myself, if you're staying here.'

Keith nodded. 'I've got to search some samples for clues.'

'And later,' Molly said, 'shall we make a special effort to get an early night?'

Next morning, while Keith was loading his suitcase into the car and adding a shotgun (not that he was expecting anything more untoward than an impromptu shooting invitation), Mrs Heller was taking a phone call from Mr Green of the Granton and Green agency.

'You wanted to think it over,' he said. 'Have you thought?'

'I've thought,' she said, thinking hard.

There was a pause on the line. 'Well?'

Mrs Heller felt her way carefully. This kind of negotiation could have a substructure of logic, almost of mathematics. 'You know my figure,' she said.

'You know mine.' The Glasgow-Irish voice was hesitant, she thought.

So he was more anxious to do business, and less sure that he held all the cards. It could be, she thought, that some new factor had made his need for the money paramount. More probably he could see his chance of a deal slipping away. Why, she wondered, would that be? 'I have my own investigators at work,' she said. 'I expect to know your client's name any time now. Meantime, if those boys of yours pull any more illegal stunts I'll make a complaint to the fuzz.'

'That could be unwise.'

'It could be unwise to let them get out of hand.' She was still fishing for the lever she needed. 'You're responsible. They're your agents.'

There was a silence on the line. Then Mr Green sighed. 'You send your boy over with five grand and I'll give you the name of my ex-client.'

70

'Ex?'

'Yes. I've got to tell you this, got to go on record to protect myself. Anything they do from here on is on their own responsibility. They're useful operatives, mind, but rough. I've had to hold them in check, and only use them for special jobs in tough neighbourhoods. But now they've made their own deal with ... my client. They're working for him direct and I'm out.'

'That should pull the price down,' she said.

'No way! You need that information more than ever. Get it and you can do your own deal with the client. Otherwise, those boys can play rough, especially if there's big money in it for them.'

'*Is* there big money in it for them?'

'There should be. If there isn't, they're being done. I was offered a ten-grand bonus if I could get proof of what happened. My advice is to send your boy Calder over with the five. And tell him to be careful.'

'I might do that,' she said. 'And again I might not. Do *they* know that I'm using Mr Calder?'

Green laughed mirthlessly. Even his laugh had accent. 'They told me. While they were watching your place, but before they got in to plant the bugs, they saw him visiting. They might have thought he was just another client, but Cyril had seen Calder giving evidence in a firearms case. Then suddenly Calder's shop was shut for four weekdays.'

She broke the connection and pressed down the switch on her intercom. 'I want to speak to Mr Calder now,' she said. 'If you can't get him, put him through the moment he phones. And tell Wally James.'

By the time his phone started ringing Keith was on his way. There were road-works on Soutra, so he was heading across country to pick up the A7. As he drove, he hummed in tune – more or less – with the car's radio. It was playing Beethoven's Fourth Symphony, not the easiest of hums.

Keith was not surprised to see the large, grey Citroen beside the road with its bonnet up. It had passed him a few minutes before at a pace that had made him wonder how long any car could stand up to that sort of punishment. The driver was out in the road waving him down, a large man with a friendly smile.

Keith pulled in behind the Citroen and wound down his window. 'You want help?' he asked.

'Help is just exactly what we want,' the man said. The friendly smile had vanished. He put an arm through the car window and plucked out the ignition key. Keith's engine died. The radio was cut off.

Keith knew better than to duck out of a car towards a hostile man, especially one who was, he now saw, possessed of a wicked-looking cosh. Fumbling with haste, Keith wound up the window. The door was locked. His key-ring, with spare car key, was deep in his pocket, but miraculously he found it and it came clear. He stabbed at the key-slot.

The driver of the Citroen – Keith thought of the big man as the driver – dropped Keith's key into his pocket. There was a flicker of his former smile on his face. With a brisk blow he drove in the window of Keith's door so that Keith was showered with little squares of safety-glass. 'Come on out, Sunshine, he said. 'The next one's for you.'

The radio came on. The engine span but failed to catch. The big man lifted his cosh, began to swing.

There was another man on the other side of the car, but he seemed smaller and less ready. Keith started to scramble to the other side of the car. The smaller man was standing too close. Keith flung the door open and the man had to dodge back.

Keith would have rolled out of the car and come up fighting – and he had been a sturdy fighter not long since – but for one mischance. As he swung over the central tunnel, the gear-lever went up his right trouser-leg.

The cosh whipped past his right ear.

Keith threw himself out of the car. His trouser-cuff twisted, locking his ankle to the gear-lever. His face and hands came down on the tarmac. He sprawled head-down, waiting for a cosh to fall. Two pairs of feet appeared beside his face.

When it came, it was not to the back of the head but a paralysing blow between the shoulder-blades that drove the breath out of him and sent agonised messages out along his nervous system.

Four strong hands grabbed him and dragged him away from the car. His trouser-cuff had started to tear, and it ripped almost to his knee. Before he could put up even a token struggle, his arms were twisted up his back and he was being frog-marched through a gap in the roadside hedge. He twisted his head around. There was not a soul in sight. The world seemed deserted. Everyone might have gone to the moon.

Beyond the hedge was a grassy shelf and then an embankment down to a small water-meadow beside a burn that was running low. Tall trees threw wavering shadows across grass and weeds.

'This'll do grand,' said a voice behind him. 'Get the cuffs on him and we'll ask a few questions.'

Keith knew that once they had him in handcuffs he was done for. They could beat out of him any information that they wanted. Afterwards, if it suited their book, they might kill him. Such things happened in a world whose fringes he had once known. And with the thought there came back to him a precept that he had known in those days and had almost forgotten. Don't fight against the pull, use it.

As one of the men took a hand away to feel for the handcuffs, Keith dragged that arm down. He could not reach the man's genitals, but he grasped the waist-band of the man's trousers and, using the pull on his arm as a springboard, jerked viciously up. At the same time he back-heeled at the other man's shin, and connected heavily. Score so far, one squawk and a grunt of pain.

As both men heaved up on his arms, Keith launched himself up and forward in a somersault. The jerk on his arms, when it came, instead of twisting the bones out of their sockets was along the length of his arms. It wrenched his muscles but it snatched his arms out of those two deadly incapacitating grips. The jerk swung Keith half round and he landed badly and heavily, on his side and half-way down the bank. He rolled to the bottom and stumbled somehow to his feet. He felt battered and winded, but this was no time to lick wounds.

The two men were coming after him. Keith was already dis-abused of his first suspicion that he was being mugged. Now, seeing the hooked nose of the smaller man, he realised that these must be Bardolph and Warrender. The larger man, Bardolph, was

73

limping down the bank with a long stride. Warrender was more circumspect. If they had come at him together Keith's problem might have been beyond solution. As it was ... he flicked over the probabilities in his mind, and liked them not one whit. With another part of his mind he tried to calculate how much it would matter if they overpowered him and he spilled the beans. He decided that it would matter like hell.

There was still nobody to be seen.

The larger man arrived with a rush, swinging his cosh round-arm. Keith ducked under and grabbed for it before it could strike again back-handed. At the same time he lashed his boot at where he judged his back-heel had landed. The thong round the man's wrist broke and the cosh came free, but they fumbled it between them and it flew into a patch of nettles. A young rabbit bolted out, crossed the burn and disappeared. Keith envied him his speed.

Keith took a punch in the ribs and returned one, harder, to the big man's lower belly.

He had bought himself just enough time to turn on Warrender, who was moving in with the handcuffs swinging like a second cosh. Keith wanted to run, or to lie down and give up, but he forced life back into his creaking shell. He feinted a kick to the groin, and as the hands came down he put his weight into a punch. It landed too high, but it put the man down for a moment.

The bigger man was coming in again, swinging a low punch. At the top of the bank a car went by unseen, almost unheard, but Keith saw the drag of its wind in the lower branches. He blocked the punch with his elbow and struck for the jaw. Too high again, but he felt teeth break and maybe the nose. Bardolph stepped back, stumbled and fell. Keith got in one kick, but the smaller man was already getting to his feet. This could go on for ever.

The bigger man got to his knees. Keith saw his own car key lying in the grass. He snatched it up and ran for the car. If he took to the driver's seat he might get away in time or he might not, and they had a fast enough car and more than enough anger to hound him off the road. He glanced behind. They were coming already, and from the manner of their coming he knew that they were no longer pursuing an aim. They were just plain fighting.

Through the hedge and onto the road. There was nobody in

sight. He dashed to his car, fumbling with the key in his left hand while he dug in his pocket with the other. He was wearing his invariable short shooting-coat and, as usual, there was a handful of cartridges loose in the pocket. The boot-lid clunked up. Keith was not a believer in gunbags, except when the law insisted, believing that their dank interiors fostered rust. His favourite double gun lay open on a nest of old coats that sometimes doubled as a backseat dog-bed. He slid the cartridges in before lifting the gun, closing it in the same motion. The radio played on. God, were they still in the short second movement?

The two men burst through the hedge and stopped dead in the face of the gun. There was a frozen moment while three sets of lungs heaved, three hearts pounded.

The bigger man, Bardolph, still had his wits about him despite the blood on his face. 'You've not had time to load,' he said indistinctly.

'You want to bet your life on it?' Keith asked.

The answer seemed to be affirmative. The man took a pace forward.

The gun was a McNaughton of top quality, far too good to use as a club. Keith could have blown Bardolph apart, or at least taken his foot off. Shunning anything so drastic and irreversible he lowered the gun and aimed short, counting on the dual effects of surprise and of richochetting pellets.

His aim was closer than he intended. At that short range the shot, still in its shot-cup, took a semi-circular bite out of the tip of the big man's sole and hit the road under his toe. Some of its energy was lost in the tarmac, the rest lifted his foot into the air as if he had stepped on a mine.

Keith let the other man see right down the barrels. 'That was meant to take his foot off,' he said quickly. 'The next shot kills.'

Warrender looked at him dumbly. His face, which had started by reminding Keith of a Semitic bloodhound, was developing a black eye of outstanding quality. Bardolph, blood dripping from his chin, was balanced precariously on one foot and staring at the other, wondering whether this new agony was a passing pain or betokened serious injury.

Keith fumbled, cross-handed, for another cartridge, then

pressed the top-lever with his thumb. The barrels dropped, and the selective ejector flicked the spent cartridge out. From habit, he caught and pocketted it. He had the fresh cartridge in the chamber and the barrels closed before either man could move. He snapped the safety-catch forward as noisily as he could.

There was still nobody in sight.

'Back through the hedge,' Keith said. They hesitated. He wondered what the hell he'd do if they refused. 'Go, or I've no option but to kill you.'

'Can't walk,' Bardolph said thickly.

'Then hop. If you fall down I'll kill you both and stuff your bodies in the culvert.'

They turned. Keith thought that they believed him because they were capable of such ruthlessness themselves. Tenderly, the smaller man helped the other to limp through the hedge and back down the bank. Keith steered them to the base of a sturdy tree which forked about seven feet above the ground. 'Sit down with your backs to that tree,' he said, and when they had complied, 'Undo your laces. Tie them again, tightly, in knots instead of bows. Now join them all together, or I'll find some other way of preventing any sudden activity. Now stay put.'

Keith searched among the weeds until he found the cosh and the handcuffs. The cuffs were of a common American design. He had stocked similar ones in the shop. Gun-collectors often branch out into military or police equipment. 'On your feet,' he said. He tossed the handcuffs to the smaller man. 'Cuff yourselves together, through that fork.'

Cursing and arguing but taking no chances on Keith's good nature, they obeyed. A whole string of lorries rumbled by on the road above. Keith laid down his gun. He could feel his knees trembling. Yet, now that it was over, he felt disappointment. Sometimes he chafed at the prosperous life that he had built for himself and hankered for rougher days gone by.

He searched the two men, ignoring their protests. They seemed to be carefully devoid of identification but well equipped. He found bugging devices, picklocks and other small housebreaking tools, a miniature camera, small, folding binoculars, but no notebooks. The only paper that they had between them was the stock of currency in the smaller man's wallet.

'How much would you reckon a broken window in my car?' Keith asked. 'Twenty-five quid?'

Warrender's face, damaged as it was – the eye was almost closed already – produced a parody of a smile and he spoke for the first time. 'To you, fifteen,' he suggested. His voice was London, Cockney Keith thought, with perhaps a hint of Hebrew.

'You can still joke, can you?'

'Not a lot.' Warrender lapsed into cautious silence.

Bardolph was chuntering on with mixed complaints and epithets. Keith ignored them and spoke to Warrender, who seemed the more intelligent of the two. 'You're from the Granton and Green agency,' he said.

Warrender's face tried to hide his consternation and calculation. 'We're on our own,' he said. 'Now,' he added reluctantly.

'Then I expect Granton and Green'll be glad to get these bits and pieces back through the post. You're Cyril Warrender, and this is Jim Bardolph. Right?'

Warrender hesitated and then nodded.

'Who's your client?'

'You can't expect that!' Warrender said quickly.

Keith paused and took a calculating look at the pair of them. Even after a fight, and almost hanging by one wrist, Warrender looked dapper. Bardolph was, in the words of Charlie the porter, 'a scruff'. Keith concluded that Warrender supplied the brains and Bardolph the muscle. He spoke to Warrender. 'You're not getting the picture,' he said. 'I don't want any more interference from you, I don't want to have to keep looking over my shoulder, and I don't want any threats. If I've got the name of your client I can get you called off by fair means or foul –' Keith had no way of knowing how closely he was paralleling Mrs Heller's argument to Mr Green '–but otherwise I'll have to put you out of action. Four broken kneecaps should just about do the job. It's wonderful how a limp in both legs slows a man down – and makes him easy to describe. Take your choice.'

Bardolph, still cursing, switched from the general to Keith in particular, but his remarks were so improbable that Keith let them pass him by. 'Not on your fucking life,' Bardolph finished.

Keith swung the cosh experimentally against his hand. It was heavy and hard, intended to injure as much as to subdue.

'I'll tell you,' Warrender said quickly.

'Shut your gob, you wee blether. He's giving you the glaiks.'

'He's what?'

'Bluffing,' roared Bardolph. 'He's just bluffing. He'd not dare.'

Warrender fell silent, waiting.

A few years before, Keith might easily have carried out his threat, but time had softened him. Despite the pain between his shoulders and the bruises on his ribs, he could not bring himself to cause a serious injury in cold blood. But perhaps a sharp rap over the knee with the cosh ... He stepped forward.

Warrender swallowed, audibly. 'Bluffing he ain't,' he said.

'He is, I tell you.'

So Warrender was the weaker vessel. Without comment, Keith addressed the cosh to the man's kneecap. 'Humbert Brown,' Warrender yelled before the blow could fall. Bardolph cursed him for a "feartie", which satisfied Keith. The two men were unlikely to be so good a team as to substantiate each other's lies while choosing between physical danger and financial loss.

'Humbert Brown?' Keith said. He remembered seeing the name on lorries, and on building sites. 'The contractors? What are they after?'

'Buggered if I know. It's true,' Warrender added quickly, cringing away for the few inches possible. 'They told us to find out what happened at Millmont House, Sunday night a week past. They said two men set off to go there, one of 'em called Harold Fosdyke. They were going to ask for a bird by name of Hilary. One of 'em hasn't been seen since, maybe both, they weren't sure.'

'What are the men's real names?'

'I dunno that either. They said to investigate the Millmont House end first, an' if we needed to know more after that we might get told.'

'And who in Humbert Brown told you all this?'

'Just a voice on the phone. We called up to offer a better deal than Green'd give.' Warrender leered deprecatingly. Clearly business was business. 'We was put onto a voice, that's all.'

Keith thought it over. It sounded probable. If there was a major

78

scandal brewing, the less that was known to a pair of disreputable turncoats the better. He gathered up the equipment from their pockets and turned away.

'You're not going to leave us like this?' Warrender said incredulously.

'What'd you have done to me, if we were the other way round?' Keith asked. 'Think yourselves bloody lucky I'm leaving you in such good shape. If one of you can't climb through that fork, just hang about until somebody comes along with enough patience to find the keys for you.' He threw the keys of the handcuffs, and the Citroen's keys, into a bed of nettles. 'Or you can starve to death for all I care. But I'll tell you this. If you've lied to me you'd better be gone before I've time to come back, or you'll be walking on four soggy stumps.'

He turned away again. Behind him, Bardolph spoke viciously. 'You bugger of hell,' he said. 'You better get home and guard that wee'n good. Because I'll get fitside wi' you one day, see if I don't.'

Keith stopped and turned. His bowels seemed to have turned to cold fire and his fists had clenched until they hurt. He waited a full half-minute until clear speech came to him. 'I'm truly sorry,' he said. 'But you've just talked yourself out of a pair of kneecaps.'

Seven

From a callbox in a small village near Eskbank, Keith phoned Mrs Heller. The cramps were easing out of his neck and stomach by then, but his hands were still shaking and when Mrs Heller came on the line he found that his voice was unsteady. 'I've just had a run-in with the two men from the Granton and Green agency,' he said.

'Are you all right? I'm warned that they're dangerous.'

'I'll do. Better than them. Their client's Humbert Brown, the big contractors. If you let them know that the men dropped their name, that'll maybe break their contract.'

'Leave it with me. I've got some pull.'

'They were rough,' Keith said, 'but in the end I was rougher. It could be called criminal assault. I just might need an alibi.'

'Any witnesses?'

'None.' Keith hoped that he was right.

There was a pause of no more than a few seconds. 'Where are you speaking from?' Keith told her. 'Right. You called in past our finance house in Edinburgh, asking for a further loan. You saw Mrs Graham. She's fat and forty, with glasses. You were there from ten until after eleven ...' She spoke on, detailing the discussion off the top of her head. It was an impressive performance.

'Did I get my loan?' Keith asked hopefully when she had finished.

'No, you did not.'

When Keith was off the line she phoned Humbert Brown and asked to speak to a Mr Howarth. He was unavailable. She left a message asking him to call her back on a matter of urgency.

Keith changed his trousers in the back of the car.

The house was deserted and it was mid-afternoon before Keith traced Mr J. M. Scott of Perth. He turned out to be the proprietor of a busy ironmonger's shop and the secretary of a shooting club, but he would have made three of the man in the photograph and

Keith remembered seeing him at a clay pigeon shoot a few months before.

Initially he was hostile, under the impression that Keith was enquiring into possible breaches of the Firearms Act. When he realised that Keith was merely seeking to return a lost camera, he spoke freely.

'I remember the Kentucky kit,' he said. 'I made it up and took it out, whyles. I didn't hit muckle, it was like trying to swat midges with a rolling-pin. So I swapped it.'

'Who to?'

'Nobody I knew. He turned up at an informal shoot we had on a local farm, for muzzle-loaders only. I don't know who brought him. He fancied the Kentucky, and he had an original double-flintlock by Bowls of Cork which was too small for his liking. It's only twenty-eight bore. I rather fancied it. I gave him a whacking great cash adjustment, but it was worth it. I've been using it to shoot rats. Grand sport.'

Keith produced the photograph.

'Yon's the lad. And that's the gun. I was almost sorry to part with it. I'll maybe build another.'

'They discontinued the kit,' Keith said. 'You've no idea who he was, or where he was from?'

Mr Scott scratched his bald head. 'I mind he said something about Dundee.'

Keith shrugged. Dundee is a sizeable city, but its shooting community is small.

When Colin Howarth called Mrs Heller back he sounded puzzled, but he was more worried. 'Is it about your swimming pool?' he asked. He hoped very much that it was no more than that.

'No. You've got that job and you'll finish it,' she said grimly. 'Or else. I've read the contract.'

Howarth felt himself come out in a cold sweat. The only other project in which the redoubtable lady had an interest in common with Humbert Brown was large and at a very sensitive stage. 'My dear Mrs Heller,' he said smoothly, 'I believe you. How can I help you?'

She punched her words in like hammer-blows. 'Your firm sent

two men from the Granton and Green agency to snoop around here. They bugged my room and the closed-circuit television, tried to pump one of my girls and a porter, and threatened an agent of mine.'

Behind his breastbone, Howarth's ulcer began to glow. Whatever he said now would be wrong. 'I don't know about any such thing,' he said carefully.

'Then you'd better bloody well find out and quick. We're part of the client syndicate you know, and if we throw our weight in against you –'

'Please,' Howarth broke in. He swallowed, hoping that some of his excess saliva might help quench the hot coal in his gut. 'Let's not even think about such a contingency. I'm sure somebody's taking our name in vain, but I'll find out for sure. Just tell me how I can satisfy you.'

'You can tell me what it is that your firm wants to find out.'

'Even if I could, I couldn't tell you. I don't suppose you understand –'

'I understand perfectly,' Mrs Heller said.

'Oh. Mrs Heller, I'm only guessing. But I've heard whispers on the company vine. I don't know that your visitors have anything to do with what I've heard, but I do know that our staff are trying to learn more about some unspecified events in order to hush up a potential scandal if it exists. So, if the matters are the same, our interests are likely to be identical …'

'Our interests are almost certainly absolutely adverse,' she said, 'and I'm not prepared to haggle one damn bit. I can afford to talk to the police, because not one of my people has stepped outside the letter of the law –' except Keith Calder, she told herself, who could do his own worrying '– whereas your agents have committed a whole series of illegal acts, and they've admitted working for you. So you'd better call them off, or prove to me that they are, as you said, taking your name in vain. Otherwise, if they or anybody else that I can trace back to you comes sniffing around here, or molests any of my people, I'll scream for the police so loud I'll give them a headache and you too. And then I'll tell the project committee that if they even allow you to tender, if anyone even mentions your name, we'll jerk out our finance. And a very good day to you.'

If Keith could have reached Dundee before the shops closed, he would have started with a round of his fellow-gunsmiths. But he met the rush of homegoing traffic in Perth Road. He swept along Riverside Drive with the wind beating in through his broken window and confounding the radio's attempts at a faithful repro- duction of the Dissonance Quartet. A private plane was touching down on the small airport. He turned up Roseangle towards the heart of the town.

A small garage was preparing to close, but they promised to replace his window for him first thing in the morning. He lugged his suitcase to the Angus Hotel, booked a room and ate a thought- ful meal.

Back in his room, Keith started telephoning. His first few calls were abortive. A phone was unanswered, somebody wasn't expected home for another hour and a lady was abroad on holiday.

He tried his home number and Molly's voice came sweetly over the line. 'I shan't be home tonight,' Keith said. 'Probably tomorrow some time.'

'All right.' She sounded disappointed but she kept anxiety out of her voice. 'How's business going?'

'I'm making progress, but I'm making enemies. I don't want them trying to get back at me through you. Could you go and stay with Janet and Wallace for a day or two?'

Molly asked no questions and expressed no surprise. Keith had made enemies before, but she had a sublime faith in his ability to triumph. Besides, a little umbrage kept him out of mischief. 'They don't have much room,' she said, 'and there's two of me now. Would it do if I got my brother to come and stay here?'

'Ronnie's back home is he?'

'Just today. I'll ask him, then. And, Keith, if there's trouble, do I call the police?'

'Good question.' He thought about it. 'Call them if you must but say as little as possible. I've been a wee bit rough. They started it, but the law might not see it that way.'

'All right. Keep your nose clean,' Molly said, 'and everything

83

else. By the bye, my bag came back through the post today. Nothing missing, no message, postmarked London. See you tomorrow, then. And I'll expect you on top of your form, the morn's night.' It was a delicate warning to him. A reduction in his sex-drive would not pass unnoticed.

Keith's next call made contact with a one-time shooting crony. 'I'm at the Angus,' Keith said. 'I don't have a car. Would you like to join me for a dram?'

Tony Carter had never been one to refuse such an invitation. 'Toot the flute and bang the drum,' he said, 'Look out the window, here I come.' Not quite as good as his word, he arrived within ten minutes and was nearly refused entry to the hotel. Keith had forgotten how badly-dressed Tony invariably was; by comparison, the scruffy Jim Bardolph was almost elegant. Anyone might have mistaken Tony for a worker in heavy industry just coming off shift – until he spoke. He had a Cambridge degree in chemistry and a Harvard degree in business management.

They chatted for a few minutes about cartridges, the Game Fair, the year's grouse prospects and the price of whisky before Keith produced his photograph of Don Donaldson. 'Can you tell me anything about this lad, or put me in touch with someone who can?'

Tony glanced at the photograph. 'I think he's away on holiday just now.'

'You know him?'

'Of course I know him,' Tony said, laughing. 'I'd know him even if I didn't shoot with him about once a fortnight. Everybody around here knows him. His face is in the *Courier* just about every week.'

Keith looked up at the tiled ceiling for a moment. 'You mean the hall porter could have identified him for me, without my having to hang around buying you doubles of the most expensive whisky ever distilled?' (Tony took the hint and ordered another round). 'Come into a quiet corner and tell me everything you possibly can about him.'

They established themselves at a quiet corner table. 'Of course,' Keith said, 'if he's a friend of yours ...'

'Not to call a friend.' Tony Carter shrugged with his hands.

84

'And I can't tell you anything that you couldn't find out by asking around for ten minutes. His name's Donald Illingworth. He's a bachelor, which is a pity – we should breed a few more of his type around here. He's an engineer.'

'Which kind? Civil, mechanical, structural or what?'

'Civil. A builder of roads and sewers. He has a one-horse private practice here, but he doesn't get much work locally – the big noises hate his guts and the builders are scared to employ him. But he's supposed to be pretty good, gets a lot of work further afield and gets called as an expert witness sometimes.

'He's a keen shooting man. I see him at the clay pigeons almost every meeting. He shoots a muzzle-loader as well, but mostly he turns up with a rusty old Spanish side-by-side that does a double discharge almost as often as it misfires. He says it's the only gun that he can hit things with, but you wouldn't know it because he's badly co-ordinated. More lead goes up than birds come down. He has a share in a small and impoverished syndicate that shoots a couple of farms. They release about two pheasants a year both of which wander straight over the boundary, but they have a lot of fun.'

'None of that sounds like much to get in the papers,' Keith said. 'What's so newsworthy about him?'

'Ah. He has a bee in his bonnet about the local sport and pastime. You may remember, Keith, that on wet Sundays, when in other parts of the country they're playing golf or swapping wives, we around here go in more for civic corruption. It's less fun but more profitable, which is what counts with the locals.'

'Don't be cynical,' Keith said. 'Just go on about Illingworth.'

Tony fiddled with his glass. 'To understand him, you've got to know a little of his background,' he said. 'A strict, religious upbringing in a gloomy old ban of a house hung with swords and flintlocks, the kirk twice on Sundays and babies the result of immaculate conception. Mother from one of the Western Isles – you know how strict they can be – and father a pillar of the local community, kirk elder, town councillor and all that. Then, about fifteen years ago – I was in the States at the time, and young Donald was just finishing college – there was a big scandal. Not the first nor the last, but this time Donald's father was slap bang in the middle of it. He and a building contractor and some others were convicted of fraud, corruption, conspiracy, embezzlement. Everything short of committing buggery with a pig, and from what I remember of the old man I wouldn't have put that past him. Old man Illingworth went to Perth Prison and died there.

'All this was very traumatic for a youngster doing his last year of studying. Mrs Illingworth went back to her croft or whatever, but Donald stayed and finished his course. Not unnaturally, he reacted violently against his upbringing. He blamed his mother for the crash – not without some justification, because she liked to keep up a bit of style, and her poor sod of a husband was only a grocer in a small way of business. So Donald cut himself off from the family, put his plate up here and stuck it out. His characteristics seem to follow with the inevitability of a psychiatric textbook. He rejected religion and all notions of conventional morality. He also developed a mistrust of women, and he's always avoided strong personal ties with them. Those two things together turned him into the local tom-cat. A bit like you used to be if you don't mind my saying so, Keith.'

'I'm a happily married man now,' Keith said mildly.

'Then there's hope for him yet. But he also rejected hypocrisy He's fairly rubbed the town's nose in some of his amours. But on the other hand he became compulsively honest.'

'Genuinely honest?' Keith asked.

'I don't think there's any doubt about it. He's the sort of fellow who borrows a couple of cartridges from you at a shoot and then follows you around for weeks, trying to give them back. His enemies have tried to discredit him for years, but they could never make anything stick.'

'Enemies?' Keith pricked up his mental ears.

'Yes. His honesty became fanatical. He became a crusader against public corruption.'

'Aha!' A state of covert war between Illingworth and a major contractor began to take on credibility, although it seemed to Keith that the engineer seemed to be cast more probably as the victim whereas the photograph suggested that he was the survivor.

'It didn't do his practice too much harm except locally,' Tony went on. 'Honest professional men shine in the dark around here.'

'And everywhere else.'

'Maybe. He got onto the council for a while, but he was such a bloody nuisance that I think, reading between the lines, that all the parties got together, even the Nats, and put their best men up against him to squeeze him off. Since then he's been prowling around the outskirts and running to the procurator fiscal with any bitties of dirt that he digs up. Just at the moment he's hitting the headlines with allegations about the Firth Bay project, but he can get just as uptight over a can of paint for a councillor's front door. In his own way he's done a lot of good; in fact, when he's learned a bit about the facts of politics he may become a useful lad to have around.'

Keith got up and fetched another round while he thought about it. The personality of Donald Illingworth – Don Donaldson at Millmont House – fitted the missing parts of the puzzle to perfection. Almost every detail was acounted for. 'Does Illingworth shoot small-bore?' Keith asked as he sat down.

'Not that I know of.'

'Does he have a source of spent bullets?'

'He's pally with a major in the Territorials.'

'That'll be it, then,' Keith said. 'Where does he live?'

'Illingworth? Out Invergowrie way somewhere, I think. Try the phone book.'

'If I drop you home, can I borrow your car until tomorrow morning?' Keith asked. 'I'll pay for taxis if you need to go anywhere.' ·

The telephone directory gave Donald Illingworth an address in Inchgavie. Keith drove there in Tony Carter's Granada and found an area of new dwellings, partly houses and partly two-storey flats, close to the banks of the Tay. Keith thought that Illingworth would be a fool if he didn't get down to the mud-flats after the geese. In which case there would be a magnum shotgun and heavy cartridges in the house. So, if he had to break in, Keith had better make damn sure that Mr Illingworth had not returned from his holiday abroad. On the other hand there was a high probability that he had no intention of coming back until all

87

danger was past. What, Keith wondered, would a man of compulsive honesty do if someone else were arrested for his crime?

Illingworth's home was an upper flat in a quiet cul-de-sac. From habitual caution, Keith drove round the corner. The road petered out where houses were still under construction. Keith left the car beyond the last street light and walked back. The sun was almost gone, the lamps dripping splashes of light onto the creeping greyness. The upstairs flat was dark. A Jaguar gleamed in the street below.

The bell rang audibly in the upper flat but produced no reaction. Keith moved to the door of the lower flat and plied a brass horseshoe door-knocker. The sound of a record-player, floating out sentimental guitar music, was suddenly muted, and a few seconds later the door was opened by a woman. Against the light, Keith could only tell that she was tall and well-rounded and long-haired. He stood as straight as his bruised ribs would let him and tried to look respectable.

'I'm looking for Donald Illingworth,' he said.

'He's away. On holiday.' Her voice was young, accentless.

'Would you mind telling me where?'

'Would you mind telling me why you want to know?'

If she had said "I don't know" or "Somewhere in the Med." or "Go to hell", Keith would have let the matter drop, at least as far as she was concerned. But when she answered one question with another Keith's mental signals began to light up. He put all his virility into his voice, at the same time cocking his head in little-boy appeal. 'It really is very important. And I think it may be important to Mr Illingworth that I talk to him as soon as possible,' Keith said. He wondered whether it was the truth. It would be nice to know. He handed over his business card – a calculated risk.

She studied him for a second in the light that came past her shoulder. 'You'd better come in,' she said.

The small living room was crowded with good furniture, as if she had moved from a larger house. They sat and looked at each other. She would have seen a darkly handsome man of athletic build and still fit in early middle-age. Keith saw, first, that she was wearing a wedding ring, and then that she was older than her voice, perhaps in her early thirties, but that the years had not hardened her; she still had the perfect complexion and the soft look of the pubescent girl.

'Perhaps,' Keith said, 'you'd rather I spoke to your husband?'

She half-smiled. 'You can if you like. You'll find him at sixty north, about three east. He's on an oil rig,' she explained.

In Keith's experience, this was a way of saying that she knew exactly when her husband could be expected home. Keith was prepared to bet that a virile bachelor would not live upstairs from this woman without some adultery being practised – and practised until they got it right. Assuming, of course, that they liked each other . . .

'Is Donald Illingworth a friend of yours?' he asked.

'We,' she stressed the word, 'get on very well with him.' She looked away for a revealing second, and unconsciously her hand smoothed down her skirt. She looked down at the card again. 'That's why I wanted to know who was asking about him. Is it about guns?'

'In a roundabout way,' Keith said. 'I can't tell you very much. There was an incident in the Borders last week. I've been asked to look into it, to see whether it can be resolved and hushed up without any scandal. Illingworth was there. Obviously, if I go around telling all about it then it can't be hushed up. I can only ask people to trust me.'

'Would you like a drink? Or coffee?'

If Keith had any more whisky he was going to have a grand night and regret it in the morning. 'A cup of coffee would be fine,' he said.

'I was just making some.'

When she came back with the coffee – percolated, with cream floating on the top – she had had time to think. 'I'll come part of the way to meet you,' she said. She stopped pouring and looked intently into his face. 'I had a phone call from him yesterday evening. Never mind where from, but it must have cost him a bomb. He wanted to know whether anyone had been asking questions about him. Would he have had you in mind?'

Keith thought quickly. His name might easily be mentioned. 'It's possible,' he said. 'I think he knows that I was trying to find out who was there at the time. He's more likely to be worrying about the police, but they don't know anything yet and they certainly won't be called in by my clients. What Illingworth doesn't know is that other people are making enquiries. In particular, a large firm of contractors. Well, in view of his crusade against left-handed contractual dealings I'd guess – and it's only a guess – that the contractors are much more likely to be a danger to him than I am. They could have a motive to ruin him. My clients have a motive for discretion.'

She handed him his cup and sat chewing her lip. 'Is it really that serious?' she asked.

'I think it could be. But I can't help if I'm left in the dark.'

'I suppose that's true. Well, tell me what you want to know, and if I think he'd want you to know it I'll tell you.'

'I wish I knew what I want to know,' Keith said. 'Tell me about the phone call.'

'H'm.' She sipped her coffee while she thought and then decided. 'He rang about seven last night. I thought he was stoned, but then I realised that that's how tension takes him. It was as if he's been under strain, keyed up, for a long time. I asked if his holiday was doing him any good and he said not really and we chatted about nothing, which struck me as odd when it was costing a fortune a minute and he'd be seeing me before much longer. And then he asked whether anyone had been asking about him.'

'*About* him? Not *After* him?'

'About,' she said. 'Definitely. Well, I'd taken a couple of messages for him and I read them out, but they were only shooting invitations, and to speak to the Round Table. That sort of thing. Then he said, "And nobody's been to the door that you couldn't identify?" And I said that there hadn't. Even then he span out the conversation, as if he was giving me a chance to remember and tell him something. I said "You'll still be back next Wednesday?" And he said something like "Probably, but I'll let you know". Something like that. And then, just before he rang off, he asked whether there's been any word from his family, and I said no, and that was about it.'

Keith kept his face blank and tried not to show any other signs of his sudden interest. 'What family would he mean?'

'*I* don't know. I'm only repeating what he *said*. He never spoke much about his family. I know he had a mother but he'd quarrelled with her. He was always sad about that,' she said, moist-eyed. 'It seemed to be the great conflict in him, and yet it's what drives him on. I'm sure you understand. He wants people to be worthy of his trust, that's why he hates any kind of dishonesty, and he feels that his family betrayed each other and himself. *Do you understand?*'

'He just doesn't trust anybody?'

'He doesn't even trust himself, because he isn't sure what may be in his own genes. He never asks anyone to trust him. He never even carries a credit card.'

Keith had a fleeting mental picture of a suspicious Mr Illingworth making love to this Amazon and being caught counting his testicles afterwards. 'I suppose it comes out in things like never leaving the key with somebody else – like you – when he goes away?' he suggested.

'That sort of thing.'

'Or would that be because he keeps his bits of evidence up there, about corruption in high places?'

She shook her head emphatically and then frowned. 'If I thought that, I'd be scared to sleep here alone,' she said. 'But he told me once that he keeps most of it in his head, and any hard evidence goes straight into the bank. Do you think it's true?'

'It sounds like him,' Keith said, 'but I'll ask. Where is he?'

'No,' she said. 'I'm not telling you that. I think I trust you,' she crossed her legs carelessly, 'but he asked me to tell nobody and I'm not going to do anything to increase his untrustingness.'

'It does you great credit,' Keith said. He wondered who he knew in G.P.O. Telecommunications who could trace a call for him. 'You've got my phone number, in case you think of anything you'd like to tell me; and I'll take yours in case I think of any questions you might like to answer. And if Illingworth calls you again . . .'

'Yes?'

Keith could not think of any informative message which he would care to pass through a third party. 'Beg him, in his own interests, to phone me. He can even reverse the charges.'

Walking back to his car, Keith was conscious of an unaccustomed glow of virtue. The old Keith, the notorious philanderer of a few years ago, would never have detected those signals of availability from such a source and passed them by. Since his marriage, Keith had held to his own fashion in fidelity. With mistresses of long standing he had felt no need to change established precedent, but he had made very few new conquests, and those only when he succumbed to temptation which he could honestly consider irresistible. His will-power, he thought, was increasing.

The truth of the matter lay deeper than Keith cared to admit to himself. As the father of a daughter, his role as a predatory male was open to question. Because what was good enough for him today might some day be good enough for some other male with little Deborah. Or for Deborah's husband.

Unaware of this conflict between his libido and his psyche, Keith gave himself a pat on the back and looked forward to telling Molly what a reformed character he had shown himself to be. Not too damn reformed, he admitted to himself, but reformed nonetheless.

In his reverie, he almost walked past a car newly parked under the last street lamp, some yards short of Tony Carter's Granada. It was a large, grey Citroen.

Keith retired into the shadow of a builder's hut while he thought about it. Presumably the two men had been freed, or had freed themselves. He was prepared to bet that Bardolph was not back in action, but Cyril Warrender was something else again; and he might have picked a fresh partner. Presumably he was not giving up the promised reward easily. He had not come to the door of the downstairs flat. Breaking into Illingworth's flat might have been a logical move.

Keith waited, leaning against the corner of the hut and nursing his sore ribs.

Warrender was taking his time. Searching a flat without revealing his presence would be a slow business. But, Keith thought, perhaps he was visiting the flat downstairs and giving the lady a hard time. Well, the lady would just have to take her chance. Keith came cautiously out of the shadows. He jammed a broken match into one of the Citroen's tyre-valves so that the tyre began to deflate, and then moved to a new hiding place from which he could see the front doors of the flats. If Warrender came out of the wrong door, Keith would know what information to beat out of him.

But, at long last, it was out of the door from the upper flat that Warrender came, walking softly and avoiding the spillage of light. With even greater caution, Keith moved through the rubble on a parallel track until he was back in the shadow of his hut. He waited while Warrender found the flat tyre and cursed, waited while he changed the wheel clumsily in the dark, waited still while he put the tools away. Warrender could have a new partner who might be standing silently in different shadows across the road. Only when Warrender was unlocking the driver's door did Keith emerge. He came up behind Warrender, his right fist already raised, and tapped him on the shoulder with his left hand.

Warrender span round. Even in the poor light of the remote lamp, the shiner that screwed his left eye shut stood out like a cowpat in the snow. With all his might, Keith punched him in the other eye. Warrender slammed back against the car and sat down hard. He leaned back tiredly against the Citroen. 'What did you do that for?' he asked plaintively.

'Would you rather I'd called the police? Or broken your knee-caps like your pal Bardolph?'

Warrender fingered his eyes, and then rested his elbows on his knees. 'You didn't break both Jim's kneecaps,' he said. 'Only one of 'em. Kneecaps don't break that easy. I'll show you some time.'

'I'll get his other one next time round. You, you're following too damn close on my heels. You'll find it more difficult with both eyes bunged up, *that's* what that was for. What did you find in Illingworth's flat?'

Warrender hesitated and then shrugged. 'Nothin'.'

Keith sighed. 'Turn out your pockets,' he said.

'Now look 'ere –'

'I've only got to wait until your other eye shuts,' Keith pointed out. 'Or stamp you flat. Either way I can go through your pockets in my own good time. I'm not feeling too kindly to you just now.

93

You held out on me this morning. You knew bloody well who Illingworth was.'

Warrender had his own grievance. 'Bloody ages we was hung on that tree,' he said. He pulled himself to his feet and emptied his pockets onto the roof of the car. Since that morning he seemed to have acquired nothing new except a few pieces of bent wire and a strip of plastic – for house-breaking, Keith presumed. There was still no notebook.

'Kick your shoes off,' Keith said, stepping back.

'I'll see you –'

'Kick them off, or I'll jump on you.'

Warrender stooped to untie his laces. As he did so, he broke wind loudly. He kicked the shoes to Keith. 'Sorry about that,' he said. 'It's always like that when I get nervous.'

A piece of paper showed white in one of the shoes. Keith picked it up and turned it to the light. The paper was folded, but the opening words caught and held his eye.

Bernera. Tuesday. My Dear Boy . . .

'If that's the way it takes you,' Keith said absently, 'you'd better not go down in a –'

The blow took him in the solar plexus before he could say 'Diving suit.' It caught him unprepared. Given warning he could have ridden the blow, but with his muscles relaxed it drove the breath out of him and paralysed the nerve-centre that controlled his breathing. He folded to the ground, slowly suffocating.

Cyril Warrender pushed his feet back into his shoes and tied the laces carefully. Then he walked to where Keith lay on the ground and kicked him hard in the face.

By the time that Keith was taking any interest in the world again, the grey Citroen was gone.

94

Eight

Keith lay on the bed in his impersonal room in the Angus Hotel, holding a bag of ice to his upper face with one hand (the floor waiter had been sympathetic) and the telephone to his ear with the other. The bell was ringing in the flat in Newton Lauder.

Wallace answered the phone at last. 'How are you getting on?' he asked.

'Did you read the top right-hand headline in the *Scotsman* this morning?' Keith asked.

'Not yet but … I'm looking at it now. I got you.'

The headline had referred to revelations by a Dundee councillor that the city's Craigowl exchange was being used for telephone-tapping on an international scale.

'It looks as if somebody'd better get over to the Western Isles,' Keith said. 'I've had a bit of a knock. Could you go?'

'It doesn't sound like my sort of trip. This isn't just because you're afraid of flying?'

'No it is not,' Keith snapped. 'I've been kicked just above the nose, and both my eyes are closing.'

'How's the other fellow?'

'Pretty much the same by now. But Warrender's a determined sort of sod, so you'd better get there first.'

'We'd best meet and talk,' Wallace said. 'I've got something to tell you.'

'You'd better come to me, and don't hang about. I don't think I could drive, not safely. I've got a blinding headache and I'm seeing double. I was going to ask you to send Molly up by train to drive me back.'

'I'll work something out. Tell me where you are and I'll either call you back or come.'

Keith was roused from an unstable sleep by a voice and then by a soft form reclining beside him on the bed and tender kisses on his

95

bruised face. 'You sound like Wallace but you feel like Molly,' he said. 'Which are you?'

He felt Molly laugh shakily against him. 'Who did that to you?' she asked. 'What a lousy thing to do! I'll scratch his eyes out.'

'Don't bother. I'd just given him a poke that'll close his other eye for a week – I'd already closed the first one – which is probably what gave him the idea. It was probably quits when I got careless. All the same, I'll tie his long nose in a knot if he comes near me again. Is it morning already?'

'It's not even midnight,' Molly said. 'Wal brought me up in a helicopter.'

'One that Personal Service often hires, in connection with business,' said Wallace's voice.

'It's waiting down at Riverside. I'd never been up in one before. It was noisy, but I did enjoy myself,' Molly said wistfully. 'You can see everything.'

'When I fly, I don't want to see anything,' Keith said. 'And don't set your heart on a chopper; we'll never afford one, and they scare me witless.' He moved uneasily and groaned. 'God! Where's my ice-bag?'

He heard water slosh. 'It's all melted,' Molly's voice said. 'Shall I get some more ice?'

'Please.' He heard the door open and close. 'Has Big Ears gone?'

'You'd be in trouble if she hadn't.'

'I was going to say I meant you. What've you told her so far?'

'Roughly the facts. But not the – er – nature of the establishment.'

'Right. Listen, now.' Quickly, Keith recounted the events of the day. 'I don't know,' he finished, 'why Warrender should think that the mother's letter was important, but then I don't know what was in it. And I don't know what he may have seen in the place and not bothered to take away with him. I was going to bust in there and take a look for myself, but I can't do it with my eyes bunged up. Wal, couldn't you –'

'Put it right out of your mind.'

'Well, if we're still in the dark after my eyes are open again, I'll come back. Or if it becomes urgent we can hire somebody. It still seems to me that you'd best go over and see Mrs Illingworth, who wrote to him on an unspecified date from Bernera, which I seem to remember's an island off the coast of Lewis. Or possibly of Harris. I suppose she lives there, but God knows and it's for you to find out. Thing is, Warrender may be on his way over in front of you.'

'Unless he can afford to hire a chopper,' Wallace said, 'he'll be behind me. There isn't a plane until morning, and even if he charters one he'll have to come down at Stornaway Airport – I don't see a charter pilot sitting down on some beach in the dark. Then he'll have to hire a car, and Gaelic doesn't have any word as urgent as *mañana*.'

'If you get there first, stay ahead. I put his mate into hospital, but he may have picked a new partner by now. Maybe you'd better take Ronnie along as a bodyguard.'

He heard Wallace chuckle. 'I'd get into more bother with Ronnie along. I use my head, not my fists.'

'Just about as hard,' Keith admitted. 'If you can track Mrs Illingworth down, find out whether anyone's been asking questions about her baby boy in the last few days. Or in the last few months, come to that. And whether he's been in touch with her. And be canny, Wal. If she gets a hint he's killed somebody she'll hold her wheest or go screaming to the police, whichever way it takes her.'

'Yes.' Wallace hesitated. 'You're sure he's the culprit?'

'Somebody got hurt, and he's still walking around. I suppose it's just possible that he's carrying around a minor flesh-wound, but I have my doubts. I'm still hoping that "Harold Fosdyke" may turn up as walking wounded.'

'Uh-uh,' said Wallace's voice. 'If that's your hope abandon it. This may change your thinking. Debbie Heller followed up your advice. She had the gardeners scouring the grounds. One of them found a dug patch deep in the shrubs not far from Chalet Sixteen.'

'They've opened it up?' Keith asked wearily.

'Yes. It contained – still contains – one dead body, male, answering Hilary's description of "Fosdyke". Hilary hasn't seen it yet; Debbie couldn't trust her to stay dumb for ever. But there's no doubt about the description. There's a hole clean through the neck, you'll be gratified to hear. Nothing in his pockets.'

'Goddam!' Keith felt a sadness settle over him, not for the

97

deceased Fosdyke but for Illingworth. Keith had been aware of a distant affection for the builder of roads and sewers. 'Is the gardener trustworthy and loyal?'

'She should be. She's an ex-tart, outlived her attractiveness. Most of the domestic staff are in that category. They never talk to the cops. Not that it matters,' Wallace said. 'I suppose this hardens your attitude? You want to lay this in Munro's lap now?'

Keith pondered and then shook his head slowly and carefully. 'Yesterday, that's what I'd have wanted. But now I'd opt for waiting until we've got all the information we can grab, before we do anything irreversible.'

'But you're the one who kept saying "Call the cops... call the cops... call the cops." I thought your needle had stuck in the groove.'

'And I may say it again. That's why I asked whether your garden-whore – Christ! What am I getting into? – could be trusted to be discreet. She can always find the body tomorrow or the next day. For the moment, I want facts. It looks bad for Donald Illingworth. If we throw him to the fuzz he'll be ruined, along with two of your companies. The young ladies of Millmont House will take a financial beating, and so'll you and I.

'Here we have a lad brought up strictly and morally. Then, just while he's at college, his parents turn out to have feet of low-grade pig-shit. Well, he could've gone either way. He develops a mistrust of personal relationships and of the morality he's been taught, so his sex-life's given over to casual affairs and to tarts. He rebounds from his old man's corruption by becoming fanatical about back-handed dealings. He sets up as a campaigner for honesty in local politics. Tilting at windmills if you like, but some windmills need to be tilted at.

'The characters in this drama, as far as we know them, seem to consist of this paragon of honesty if not of virtue, and a big contractor whose reputation isn't exactly sweet. Which horse would you back?'

'I wouldn't back any horse with a bookie who called himself Honest John,' Wallace said. He sounded amused. 'Doesn't it occur to you, Keith, that public prating about honesty often covers up more dishonesty than anything else? And that this – what did you

98

call him? – builder of roads and sewers has a lot in common with a big contractor?'

'Are you trying to persuade me to go to the police?' Keith asked. 'Have we changed roles?'

'No.'

'Tell me honestly, Wal. Aren't Humbert Brown good customers at Millmont House?'

'It's possible.'

'Orgies for councillors?'

'Such has been known.'

'Yet Illingworth hadn't been there before,' Keith pointed out. 'No, Wal, I'm inclined to give him the benefit of what little doubt there is. I think Donald Illingworth killed "Harold Fosdyke" and buried him in the garden, but I want to know why before I blow the whistle.'

Wallace sighed, loudly, for Keith's benefit. 'Knowing won't change facts,' he said. 'And his mother would be the last person to know them, or to tell me if she did.'

'She must know something,' Keith said. 'Try and find out what it is.'

'Will d-do. You can't be wrong all the time. Molly told you her bag came back through the post? She guesses that he looked inside, saw the tails sticking out of the cassettes and knew that he'd pinched a lot of unexposed film, so instead of chucking it away in a ditch like any reasonable man he spends a few quid posting it back. That at least suggests that his compulsive honesty isn't all a put-on. Well, if that's the lot I'd better be getting back to the chopper.'

'You'll land in the small hours,' Keith said. 'Better sleep here and go over at dawn.'

'You're joking!' Wallace said. 'Do you have any idea what one of those things costs to keep hanging around? I'll go over now. At least, with a chopper, you're flexible. I'll cruise around, and if I can't spot a hotel still showing lights I'll doss down in somebody's shed. The weather's still holding.'

Molly came back a few minutes later. Keith pressed the replenished ice-bag gratefully to his throbbing face. 'Has Wally gone?' Molly asked. 'Damn, damn, damn! I wanted to hear all

99

about it. Never mind, you can tell me in the car. Do you want to go down overnight, or shall we stay here. Janet said she could cope with Snooks.'

'Deborah,' Keith corrected automatically. 'We've no choice. I got a window busted in the car. If they can't replace it by lunchtime we'll take it as it is and be grateful for the air-conditioning. Can you get a room?'

'I can double with you.'

'It's a single bed, you may notice.'

'Plenty of room if we snuggle up a bit. Then I can kiss your poor face better.'

'You can try, I suppose,' Keith said. 'Just get in gently. You usually come in from fifty feet without a parachute.'

'What rubbish!'

'It is not. Being joined in bed by you comes somewhere between doing an assault-course and being raped.'

Mrs Heller phoned Mr Howarth of Humbert Brown at an hour of the morning which was early enough for him and could have been considered to be the very crack of dawn for one of her sisters in frailty. Her voice made him think of shaving with a ragged blade; it had the same keenness and the same capacity for leaving his nerve-ends exposed. His ulcer flared like a hot coal in a gale.

'Your man Warrender,' she said, 'has just tried to kick my agent's face in.'

'I don't admit that he's our man,' Howarth said, 'but we've been trying to contact him to buy him off. We can't reach him. He's travelling.'

'I suggest you cut short his travels, and quick. The joint committee meets in three days, and unless I know by then that you have absolutely no agents out I'm going to tell the committee that our finance will be withdrawn if your name's even mentioned. Good day to you!'

She hung up on his protests and left the room. One minute later, in sensible brogues instead of her usual elegant slippers, she left the house. Near Chalet Sixteen she turned off the path and picked her way between two rhododendron bushes. In the glade beyond, the young Scots Pine stood bravely against its stake like some puny martyr. It gave reason enough for the signs of disturbance on the ground. As she looked, her smooth young face took on twenty years.

She was roused by a voice filtering through the bushes from one of the many loudspeakers scattered about the grounds. 'Mrs Heller to the house, please,' it said, gruffly but politely. 'Immediate visitors. Mrs Heller to the house, please.'

"Immediate" was a code-word. It meant police.

She took her time, forcing relaxation into her mind and body as she walked. Waiting in her office she found a thin, dark man in the uniform of a senior police officer – she was vague as to the exact meaning of the badges. He was accompanied by a sergeant who lurked silently in a corner.

'I am Chief Inspector Munro,' the thin man introduced himself. 'And this is Sergeant Ritchie. I am investigating an incident or a series of incidents.' His voice was West Highland, his diction careful, as if Gaelic would still come easier to his tongue.

'Yes?'

'I am wondering whether you might not have something to tell me?'

She forced herself to smile. 'You'll have to be more specific than that,' she said. 'My life story would curl your hair.'

He looked without smiling. 'It might curl what little I have left,' he agreed. 'Has anything more than usually unusual happened here during, say, the past week?'

'Nothing,' she said.

'Do you know a Mr Calder? Keith Calder?'

She kept her face still and hoped that the muscles around her eyes were giving nothing away. 'The gunsmith? He overhauled and valued a collection of antique guns that we bought.'

'Have you seen him recently?'

'He came here the day before yesterday, to value a pistol for me.'

'Is he doing anything else for you?'

'No.' She tried to time the word, neither too quick nor too slow.

'M'hm.' Munro opened his case. He laid a photograph on the

desk in front of her. 'Have you ever seen this man?'

'No,' she said. To her own ears her voice sounded too quick. The picture was a poor Polaroid shot of the snooper who had confronted her in this room. He seemed to be wearing pyjamas and an expression of suppressed fury. 'Not that I remember.'

'You would see a lot of men here.' Munro laid down another photograph. 'And this one?'

'No.' Her mouth was dry. She remembered not to moisten her lips, nor to sit too still. The photograph showed the man whose body lay near Chalet Sixteen. He was laughing with a woman in the garden of a small house.

The shocks were coming too fast. Her head swam. She wondered whether to buy time by letting herself faint. But a faint would be an admission. She pushed a pencil off the desk, bent to pick it up and held the position until her head cleared. Quick as light, during the process of straightening up and laying down the pencil, her mind flitted over facts and suppositions. She thought:

The bastard knows what we do. What else does he know?

Humbert Brown wouldn't have told the fuzz a word.

He doesn't know about the body. The man's wife may have reported him missing.

He wouldn't have told his wife where he was going. They never do. Not even the man who comes about the rates. Especially him, come to think of it.

But the man's wife might know the general area he was going to. That would be enough for this bugger to bring along that photograph. Does he know there's a connection between the two?

If he does, I can't see how.

So what put him on to us?

That damned private dick.

Calder shouldn't have put him in hospital.

Should I cancel that alibi? Let Calder go down?

The man may have talked in shock. Spur of the moment. Would he go on talking?

Does he know anything to matter?

Probably not. He was fishing in the pool where the fish swam last, but he didn't catch more than a tiddler. His mate may have hooked something bigger since then, but he wouldn't know about that.

Would he?
I'm glad Calder put the bastard in hospital.
Can this copper be sure that either of them ever came here?
Probably not.
Probably? Was somebody watching them watching us?
'Is it important?' she heard her voice ask.

Munro hesitated while he scratched his nose. 'Very important,' he said.

Debbie Heller was expert at reading a man. *He doesn't know,* she thought exultantly. 'Leave the photographs with me,' she said. 'I'll find out whether anybody here has ever seen either of them.'

'I wish to interview them myself.' Munro flushed darkly and avoided the amused eye of his sergeant.

Nice try, she told herself. But the staff were well briefed and Hilary had been sent away for a few days respite. 'You do, do you?' she said. 'We'll see them together. I'll call them in at five-minute intervals.'

'And I want to see your list of appointments for the past week. You do keep a list?'

'We do not operate off a street corner,' she said coldly. 'Is this in confidence, outside of whatever it is that you're after?'

'You have my word.'

'And whatever you're after, it isn't just to prosecute us?'

Munro shook his head. 'Again, you have my word.'

'I'll accept it,' she said. 'I'll give you a print-out from the computer. But you won't find many real names. And any real names which you do find, and which aren't implicated in anything criminal, you will kindly respect.'

Munro grunted. 'They will remain confidential,' he said, 'but I will not respect them because I do not respect what you are and what you stand for. Oh yes,' he held up his hand as if to ward off an interruption, 'I know that you have helped us from time to time with word of things that have been overheard here. You have even let our men set up a listening-post. But that does not mean that you represent law and order. It does not alter the fact of what you do, and I shall never approve of it.'

Debbie Heller smiled inside. She would rather bandy moralities with the chief inspector than have to lie to him about visitors.

Keep him on the hop, she told herself. 'If you make any such suggestion about me outside this room,' she said, 'I'll sue you. I'm the chairman and managing director of a substantial group of companies. Those companies happen to include one of which you don't approve, because it makes accommodation and a secretarial service available to girls. Well, tough titty! You may not like the morals. You may even think that it offends against the law. But you'd get no support from the procurator fiscal and you know it.'

Munro's forehead had a purplish tinge. 'Because you have corrupted my fellow-officers?'

'No. Because that company exists to give the girls a chance to keep and invest their earnings over a period and then to get out of the game, as I did, instead of being milked and sweated and dominated by some member of your sex, Mr Munro, until they're old and ugly and flat broke. We probably rescue more girls from prostitution than all the social workers in the country added together.'

'That is no different from the criminal who commits his last big crime in order to retire,' Munro said indignantly, waving a boney finger at her. 'But we will never agree. Never. Now, Mrs Heller, the photographs.'

'Ah yes.' She put her finger on the intercom, and withdrew it. 'You can see the girls alone if you want.' She managed to work up a leer and put a slight emphasis on the want.

Munro was a brave officer, but his Calvinist upbringing was weighing him down. The very idea of visiting scarlet women in their boudoirs terrified him. 'No thank you,' he said.

'We give a small discount to serving officers.'

'And pensioners, no doubt,' Munro sneered.

'That question has never arisen yet.'

Nine

It was nearly noon before the window was replaced and Keith and Molly got away from Dundee.

Keith, awakening, found that he could with some difficulty crack his eyes open enough to give him a blurred and distorted view of the world, but the view was hardly worth the pain. It was easier to let Molly sponge his face, dress him and prepare his breakfast, and to wait patiently while she visited travel-agents on his behalf and then fetched the car.

In the passenger's seat, Keith leaned back against the head-rest and wondered why the position felt uncomfortably familiar. Then he remembered. When Molly drove, he always closed his eyes.

Molly started off grimly silent as she braved the traffic.

'You're going by Perth and the motorway, are you?' Keith asked after a minute or two.

'I hate that road through Fife. And I thought you couldn't see.'

'I can't. But I didn't hear you stop and pay a toll on the bridge. So what did you find out at the travel agents?'

'Just a moment.' Molly was silent again while she spurted past what sounded like a Corporation bus. 'You were right. I put on a voice like Inspector Munro and said that I was Donald Illingworth's sister.'

'Did you find out where he is?'

'Yes. I said that our mother was desperately ill and calling for him, so would they please tell me where he is.'

'And where is he?' Keith asked.

'At the first one they thought I was daft, but I struck lucky at the second. They didn't want to tell me, they said it was confidential, so I said that it was a matter of a legacy, and my brother would certainly sue them if he got cut out of our mother's will because they'd been so stubborn, and in the end they told me.'

'Where?'

'You don't have to shout. He's in Madeira. Funchal. They

showed me a brochure. It looks lovely. Keith, do you think we could go to Madeira some time?'

'Possibly,' Keith said. 'Possibly. But meantime go through Edinburgh. I want you to describe the outside of the Personal Service building to me.'

'I don't like driving in Edinburgh,' Molly said. 'Is it important?'

'I don't suppose so, but it might be.' Keith fumbled for the radio and switched it on. Jangling discords; something by Stockhausen, he thought, not the medicine for a man feeling depressed and uncertain. When they were safely on the dual carriageway he said, 'Find me a nice, soothing tape, would you? Something easy, all melody. Is the Mendelsohn violin concerto in the car?'

'You took it out. Anyway,' Molly said, 'I'd rather you told me what this is all about.'

'Wallace said he told you.'

'He thinks he did. But he was so vague and circumspect I still don't know whether you're in trouble or not.'

'I don't *think* I am,' Keith said, 'except for having quite a financial stake in solving a problem.'

'You're troubled in your mind, though. I can always tell.'

Keith eased himself into a more comfortable position. He was finding more and more parts of his anatomy that were grumbling about the activities of the previous day. 'I was asked to deal with something in absolute confidence and without scandal, so I'd be daft to blab about the details.' Keith seemed to remember saying much the same to Illingworth's neighbour the night before. He paused and sorted out his thoughts. 'I'll tell you this much, and don't you go telling a soul. I was asked to investigate because there was a bloodstain found and a lead ball. It looked as if somebody'd maybe been shot. It could have been an accident, a minor wounding or a suicide, but there could have been a murder. The other trouble was that any kind of scandal would trigger off financial losses that'd rub off on us. Even so, I was the one who wanted to call in the police; but I was persuaded to carry on until we could be sure that something really serious had happened.'

'And now?'

'Now I'm damn sure that something serious happened. But in

106

the meantime a lot of other little signs –' Keith broke off. 'No, not signs,' he admitted. 'Mostly hunch. Crystal ball and tea leaves. The man I had my fight with was working for a big contractor, a firm that's none too scrupulous about how they get their contracts just so long as they get them. They've figured in one or two big bribes cases. We don't know the identity of the victim for sure yet, but my guess is that he was connected with them one way or another. Otherwise I can't see any reason for their interest, not one that makes sense all the way.

'By process of elimination, the other man has to be the guilty one. And I've just found out his identity. He's a man who sets a very high standard of honesty for himself and others.'

'A pillar of virtue?' Molly sounded disbelieving.

'Not virtue,' Keith said. 'No. If, when I was younger, I'd been as much of a one for the lasses as you've always wanted to think, which I wasn't, I'd've been a babe in arms compared to his one. His private life's in one hell of a fankle.. But he seems to be a genuinely honest man. He's set his face against dishonesty, especially corruption with public funds.'

There was another break in their discussion while Molly slowed to let a faster car by and then pulled out to pass a Juggernaut. 'There aren't that many honest folk,' she said. 'The rest I could believe, but not the honest bit. You make him sound like Donald Illingworth.'

Keith felt himself jump. 'You know him?'

'It's him is it? Not to say know. He's been in the shop once or twice – he bought one of those copper powder-flasks. And I've seen him on the telly when he was making a speech about something. He looks as if he needs to put a little weight on and to relax a bit more.'

'Or a bit less,' Keith said.

'I didn't mean that. He only popped into my mind because he was at the Game Fair.'

Keith sighed. If he had only remembered to consult Molly he could have saved a day, a lot of driving, at least one fight and possibly two, the cost of a new window and the danger of being charged with assault. 'You think he's sincere?' he asked. 'Or could all that honesty be a sham?'

Molly deliberated for a couple of miles. 'I think it's for real,' she said. 'I wouldn't trust him with my grandmother in the middle of a crowd, he has that sort of look. But I don't doubt his honesty.'

'Could he be a brilliant liar? Like a secondhand-car salesman?'

'No, it's not just meeting your eye without staring, that sort of thing. I made a five pound error with his change, gave him a fiver too much. He didn't notice until he was out of the shop, but he came back. Most men would've just shrugged and smiled. No, I don't think he's two-faced, I think he's just the sort of man who'd send my films and lenses back to me.'

'That's what I thought. So while I can't see any doubt but that he shot another man, I want to know more about how and why before I do anything about it.'

'Aren't you rather setting yourself up as judge and jury?' Molly asked.

'I suppose I am. But the law is a very blunt instrument. Law and justice fit where they touch, and they don't always make a very good contact. Sometimes they need a little gumption added.'

'Mr Munro might not agree with you.'

'Humph! That canting bloody highlander still has peat between his toes. He'll have one hell of a job proving *when* I found out that there'd been a fatal shooting. I want to know why before I commit myself.'

'If he's killed somebody, nothing'll make that right,' Molly said in a small voice.

'I'd like to remind you of something. Once upon a time, somebody stuck you with a knife. I chased him up into the hills. I was going to hand him over to Munro, but first I wanted to make him wish he'd never been thought of. So I pulled my own knife, and every time he slowed down I gave him a fright that set him going again. After about three hours, he dropped dead. I told you that I hadn't meant to kill him, and you said that I *should* have meant it. All right, maybe you were just saying it to make me feel better, but there was a lot of sense in what you said. If I find that he killed out of greed or lust or spite, Munro can have him and welcome. If he turned out to be a member of a terrorist organisation, I'd think that he'd forfeited any right to membership of the human race and I'd kill him myself. But the probability is that he tilted at one windmill too many and killed a giant at last. So I want a chance to think it over if it turns out that he was striking a blow for honesty or defending the lady's honour or something.'

'There was a girl in it, was there?' Molly said.

'I didn't say so. Well, maybe I did. There was, but her part in it seems to be negligible. According to her she was away before anything happened, and her story checks out so far.'

'Really checks out? Or is this more crystal ball and tea leaves? Or a logical deduction that nobody with a swollen bust and lace pants could possibly tell a lie? I know how you think, Keith Calder.' Molly spoke lightly, but there was a trace of anxiety in her voice.

Keith started to smile, but stopped quickly when his battered face objected. 'You think you do,' he said. 'But you don't. What you're saying is that I'm a male chauvinist pig to exclude her because she's female. Equal opportunities for murderesses.'

'If you want to be silly about it.'

It was Keith's turn to be silent for a mile or two. 'Maybe you're being coaxed in the direction of female chauvinism by Illingworth's blue eyes,' he said at last. 'I don't think I'm being chauvinist. I take a realistic view of the difference between men and women.' (*By God you do!* Molly thought). 'As far as we know, the girl had no,' Keith tried to think of another word, and couldn't, 'connection with either man, she has a sort of alibi, and she drew attention to the bloodstain when she could have ignored it.'

'Go on.'

'All right, there's one other factor. This wasn't a woman's crime.'

'Aha!'

'Not "Aha!", but far from it,' Keith said.

'You're always generalising about women.'

'I don't think I'm generalising. I try not to. People exaggerate the gender differences, it's more fun that way. When you come down to it, the differences – apart from the hooray differences – are only on average. For better or worse, nature decided that your sex was going to specialise in reproduction and aftercare, and mine was going to be the provider and the defender. Some

109

creatures are quite different, but that's how it is with humans. So the average man can run faster than the average woman, but although I'm at least as fast as the average man there are some women who can run faster than I can.'

'You've found out, haven't you?' Molly said. The acute listener might have detected a nice blend of pride and concern in her voice.

'I can't be sure how hard some of them were trying,' Keith said. 'On average, man has strength and aggression, woman has gentleness, patience and endurance. I don't say that it's fair, I don't say that it's always true, but on average that's the way it is. So when you get more than one pointer, it's only a freak that runs against the pattern.

'Now, in this case somebody had to dismantle an antique pistol to get it down off the wall, produce muzzle-loading materials and load and cap it.'

'I could have done that,' Molly pointed out.

'So you could. And this particular girl at least likes old guns as ornaments because they were on her wall, but I don't think she knows a damn thing about them and she sure as hell wouldn't have had powder, a ball and a cap lying about. She might have had access to Illingworth's car, and what put us onto him in the first place was the likelihood of his having a bootful of muzzle-loading materials.'

'He could have loaded it for her.'

'He could, but I can't see any reason why he should.'

'All right,' Molly said. 'So she had access to his car.'

'Next point, guns aren't a woman's bang, if you'll pardon the pun. They don't have the same phallic connotation for a woman as they do for a man, and women aren't nature's fighters and meat-gatherers. And again, she'd have had to improvise. Illingworth's twenty-bore Kentucky is nippled for large military caps, and those would be all that he had with him. The nipple on the pistol was sized for a twenty-six cap, and there were signs that somebody had bodged up a larger cap with chewing-gum to make it fit. But women aren't at home with mechanical things; they can learn to use them, but they're never in sympathy with them. They're better with animate things, they often make better

110

dog-trainers, horse-riders and carriage-drivers than men. But a woman can only be taught to operate a machine; ask her to understand it, to improvise, and she's lost. That's why I don't think a woman did this.'

'Rubbish!' Molly said, half-laughing. 'You and your homespun philosophy! You just don't think much of us.'

Keith laughed in his turn, and winced. 'I think of you all the time,' he said. 'I think women are nice people. But I'm right about their mechanical ineptitude. That's why, on average, they don't make such good drivers as men.'

'Rubbish!' Molly said again. She pulled out to overtake.

'There you are,' Keith said. 'A man would have changed down, but you pulled away with the engine labouring. You give me a tape-recording of a driver in traffic and I'll tell you whether it's a man or a woman, and I'll back myself to be right eight times out of ten.'

'You show me a graph of his blood pressure and I'll tell you the same thing,' Molly retorted.

'You're a female chauvinist sow,' Keith said.

The argument lasted them as far as the Forth Bridge.

Keith never got the benefit of Molly's description of the Personal Service building. 'Put her along,' he said as they reached the Newbridge roundabout. 'I want to get home. I've things to do.'

'Can you do them with your eyes bunged up?'

'I can dictate some more of my book into the tape-recorder. Did I tell you I've got a good chance of laying my hands on a Ferguson Rifle? I'd like to get that bit dictated while it's still fresh in my mind.'

'Well, I'm not going to get pinched for speeding just in case you forget a bit,' Molly said rebelliously. 'There was a police car back at the roundabout.'

'They never have a radar trap here. There's nowhere to pull the offenders in that you can't see miles off. Anyway, it's de-restricted in a few yards.'

Molly speeded up slightly. 'And I don't want to cause an accident.'

'It's not fast drivers that cause accidents. Slow drivers cause

111

accidents. Fast drivers die in them, though.'

'Well then . . . Keith, that police car's following us.' There was a touch of panic in Molly's voice. The car slowed again.

'Don't crawl,' Keith said. 'That's the first thing to make them wonder about you. You're sober, I think your driving license is up to date and the car's insured for you. So shut up worrying.'

'If you say so.' Molly muttered to herself as another mile rolled away. 'Keith, they're coming up alongside. They're signalling me to pull in. What have I done wrong?'

'Nothing. There's a lay-by outside Ingliston Showground. Pull in there.'

'We're just passing it.'

'Then go down the Turnhouse slip-road.'

Molly turned down the slip-road and stopped. Keith heard another car pass them and park, and footsteps walking back. 'Mr Calder,' said a voice.

'Two ugly coppers want a word with you,' Molly said. She sounded shaky.

Keith forced up one eyelid for a second. 'You're not wrong,' he said.

The two constables had heard the exchange but remained unmoved. 'Mr Calder?' one of them said again.

'Me,' Keith said. 'The one on the left.'

'Chief Inspector Munro wants you back in Newton Lauder.'

Keith digested this information on one level of his brain while another level said, 'He's in luck. That's where we're going.'

'Were you, sir? Or were you heading for the airport?'

'I've just told you I was on the way home. We turned down here because you signalled us to stop.'

The constable's voice was disbelieving. 'Came over the Forth Bridge, didn't you? Would you mind telling me why you're on this road?'

Keith had no intention of mentioning the Personal Service building. 'If we went in by the Queensferry Road,' he said, 'my wife would have to drive in the worst of the Edinburgh traffic. No way does she do that while I'm in the passenger seat. This way we go through Gogarburn and onto the Ring Road.'

The policeman thought it over for a few seconds. It was a

perfectly valid route. 'Would you mind getting out of the car?'

'You can see that I'm injured. I think you'd better tell me what it's all about.'

The officer's voice was becoming increasingly hostile. 'Would you care to tell me how you got injured?'

'No,' Keith said, 'I would not.'

'My orders are to bring you to Newton Lauder.'

'I'm going there anyway,' Keith said patiently.

'Just come with me, please.'

'If you insist. Molly, get hold of Mr Enterkin for me. Tell him that they refuse to tell me anything.'

'Yes, of course.'

'Tell him that I'm saying nothing until I know what it's about. And tell Janet.' Janet, Keith hoped, would have the sense to get a message to Mrs Heller. 'And before I get out of the car, take a look at their warrant cards for me.'

Ten

They made good speed and no conversation. Keith passed the time by keeping mental track of their progress, but he was still placing them at the top of Soutra Hill when they made the sharp turn off the main road towards Newton Lauder. Keith's own house was somewhere off to the right. The sound of the car changed as they entered streets. They pulled up in the square.

One of the policemen took Keith's arm, and not, Keith thought, out of consideration. It was the constable who had done all the talking; Keith knew the gruff voice. Keith made what use he could of his blurred vision as they climbed the low step and entered the police building.

Mr Enterkin's voice was like the barking of an angry terrier. Keith could imagine the fat little solicitor scampering dog-like around the tiled corridors, snapping at heels. 'Which of these men did that to you?' he demanded.

Keith was sorely tempted; but medical examination would show that his bruises were sixteen hours old. 'I had a fall in the hotel bathroom,' he said. 'What sort of speed did Molly drive at, to get here first?'

'She phoned. You're not saying that because you've been intimidated?'

'No.'

'Have they been keeping you from getting medical attention?'

'I don't need a doctor,' Keith said.

'That's a matter of opinion.'

Keith could feel hands pulling at him and he managed to make out the thick-set form of Sergeant Ritchie. 'Chief Inspector Munro wants to see you right away,' Ritchie's voice said.

'Not without me,' Enterkin said.

'Mr Munro wants to see him alone first.'

'I can keep my trap shut,' Keith said.

'I'm coming along to make sure of it.'

114

'No you are not,' Ritchie said firmly. 'Come along now, Keith – er – Mr Calder.'

Ritchie pulled one of Keith's arms. One of the visiting officers jerked at the other. Keith let himself stumble. He was playing for time and a psychological advantage. He meant to save himself, but when Ritchie let go of his arm the other policeman held on. Keith swung round and as he fell he hit his nose on the counter. The blow was slight, and although it set his bruises pulsing he had many a time suffered worse in friendly tussles with Molly's brother. He need not have produced such heart-rending groans . . .

Mr Enterkin rounded on a stout woman who had been arguing over a summons for a chimney-fire. 'Madam, you were witness to that assault.'

She nodded happily. The police seldom find friendly witnesses within their own portals. 'Aye. Right coarse it was,' said the lady, 'and done on purpose too.'

'You'll testify to that?'

'So help me God.'

'Mrs McHarg, isn't it?'

Keith was on his knees. While Mr Enterkin and Mrs McHarg held their dialogue and Sergeant Ritchie protested the accidental nature of the mishap, he felt his face. The knock had set his nose bleeding and he managed to transfer some of the blood to his swellings. He could have done with a mirror, but by touch alone he was confident that he was presenting the sort of picture that Mr Enterkin could best use. 'I think I'll be all right,' he murmured bravely.

'The poor laddie!' said Mrs McHarg. 'See what they've done to him!'

'Come along now, Keith man,' said Ritchie. His careful officialese was slipping under pressure. 'You're no' sair skaithed, an' it was just a mishanter. Come away and see Munro. And nae lawyers, for the love of God.'

'If you separate me from my client even for one second,' Enterkin said grimly, 'I'll be back with a press photographer and a reporter before you can start to clean him up. The *Borders Advertiser* has an office just up the road.'

Chief Inspector Munro found himself very much at a disadvantage. In the circumstances he could hardly prise Keith forcibly out of Mr Enterkin's tenacious clasp, and having got Keith at last into his office he was forced to release him again, albeit temporarily, first into the washroom and then for the attention of a doctor who, to Munro's stark horror, expressed privately to the chief inspector his anxiety as to whether either blow, and he stressed 'either', might not have caused serious injury. The doctor mentioned detached retinae and intercranial haemorrhage among other horrors, and Munro took little comfort from the fact that the doctor was a notorious prophet of doom. Nobody, Munro felt, could be wrong all the time.

Even when he had got rid, for the moment, of the doctor and had seated Keith and Mr Enterkin in his room together with a constable to take shorthand, he found his visitors more anxious to discuss a personal suit against himself than the reason for Keith's enforced return to Newton Lauder. Almost as bad, he found his mind distracted by a concern, which he would never have admitted, for Keith. When they had first met, Keith's amorous bachelorhood, disrespect for the police and preoccupation with firearms had combined to give Munro an acute dislike of him, but over the years Munro had come to know Keith and to hold him in reluctant but firm respect. This was not going to be easy.

'Very well, then,' Munro said at last, testily. 'We have discussed it long enough. Either you are going to sue or you are not. Which is it to be?'

'These things can't be rushed,' Enterkin said. 'They take time. Evidence must be gathered, precognitions taken, counsel's opinion sought. Your own conduct during the remainder of this interview may well have a bearing. So far we have only discussed the assault which was carried out, we believe on your orders. We have yet to touch on the matter of wrongful detention. My client has been here for an hour and in the hands of your officers for twice as long, and he has still not been told the reason. His time is valuable, and mine is far from cheap.'

'That's *right*,' Keith said. 'I'll remind you that I'm –'

'If,' Munro said violently, 'you ever again tell me that you are a respectable businessman now, I think that I shall give you far better ground for litigation than you have at present. Or,' he added, 'if you say again that you are a happily married man.'

'I hardly think that my client's married status comes into this,' Enterkin said.

'Why not?' Keith asked. The imp of mischief that lived forever behind his shoulder had been tickled at Munro's discomfiture, and Enterkin had been quick to catch on and help to keep the policeman off-balance. 'He drags my past sins –'

'Alleged sins,' said Enterkin.

'–alleged past sins into everything else. I don't know why he's so determined to believe that I still stray from the straight and narrow. I've got a fine wife in good working order. I tell you, Munro, I resent these constant slurs. Enterkin, could we not get an interdict restraining him from uttering slanders?'

'Probably. Would you like me to raise an action?'

Munro pulled himself together and towered over the two men, who were lounging at ease in his hard chairs. 'I made no slurs,' he said, 'and if you tell me what you were doing yesterday I may, just *may*, be able to let you walk out of here without a charge.'

'All day yesterday?'

'Yes.'

'You don't have to say anything,' Enterkin said. 'We can walk out of here any time that you like.'

'Unless he charges me?'

'That's so.'

'But he's given me no idea what he's on about.' Keith switched his attention to Munro. 'I see no reason at all to tell you all about my day yesterday when I don't know what you're enquiring into.'

Munro thought, in Gaelic:

This is not going to be easy. When this son of an unmarried lady uses that tone of voice, he is as slippery as an eel.

But there is something going on and he is a part of it.

Men are coming and going as never before.

Two men injured and hanging from a tree, and the sound of a shot.

Two men were seen, they seemed to be watching Millmont House. They sound like the same two men.

I will start with the two men.

'Have you ever been to Millmont House?' he asked.

Keith nearly jumped. 'Mind your own damn business,' he said.

'I think you did. On business? Your business? Or theirs?' When Keith sat silent, Munro went on. 'But you will be saying that I am making slurs again. Yesterday, just before noon, two men were found handcuffed to a tree. One of them had a broken kneecap. A witness saw you driving away. What have you to say to that?'

Keith thought furiously:

Witness?

Farmer attracted by sound of shot?

I never shoot around there. Nobody local would know my face. Did he get my number? If so, did he just see me driving by?

Better not produce my alibi if I don't have to.

Would that bleeder Bardolph have talked? Named me?

Not on purpose. That sort hold their tongues.

Under an anaesthetic? Wouldn't hold up as evidence.

Without Bardolph pressing charges, there'll be no case.

Not if I keep my trap shut. Sit tight.

'I just want to say –'

'One moment,' Enterkin broke in. 'Better to say nothing at all than half a story. What you don't say can be revealing, or misleading, or downright dangerous. So wait until we've been allowed to discuss the implications in private.'

'I was only going to say that talking to the police never did an innocent man any good, let alone a guilty one. But I don't want to hang about in here waiting for a case to be brought.'

'You're not charged with anything yet. If you want to walk out of here, start walking. I could get you bail on an assault charge. Mr Munro, did your witness know Mr Calder?'

Munro set his lips firmly. 'You can't expect –'

Enterkin rose to his feet, very lightly considering his rotundity, beckoned to Keith and then realised that Keith was not responding to gestures. 'Come,' Enterkin said irritably.

'He identified him,' Munro said.

'If he didn't know him beforehand, how did he identify him?'

'From a photograph,' Munro said. (Keith said later that the words came out with as much eager spontaneity as if he'd been

118

shitting coke, and Molly said that if Keith didn't bolt his food he wouldn't know what that felt like.)

Mr Enterkin gently pushed Keith back into his chair and resumed his own seat. 'Ha!' he said. 'There goes any chance you might have had with an identity parade. The local sheriffs have strong views about policemen who show witnesses photographs of the accused and then put him in a line-up. What a pity,' he added.

'We shall see,' Munro said. 'Mr Calder, why were you making for Turnhouse Airport when the officers stopped your car?'

'I –'

'Mr Calder has nothing to say, ' Enterkin broke in. 'But I am advised by Mrs Calder, who was driving the car, that she was about to pass the slip-road for Turnhouse when the police car overtook her and she was signalled to stop. Naturally, she turned down the slip-road.'

'That is not what the two officers say.'

'Then no doubt you will take disciplinary proceedings against them. A car which had been following my client's turned down the slip-road after them and the driver, according to Mrs Calder, slowed down and took a good look at the tableau. He had three passengers.'

'Did Mrs Calder get the number of the car?' Munro asked.

'Unfortunately no. But no doubt the Police National Computer –'

'From a description?' Munro sounded half-relieved, half-disappointed. 'I hardly think it practicable.'

'A lime-green Rolls,' Enterkin said. 'How many of those do you think the computer would cough up?'

Chief Inspector Munro made no answer. His mind, reverting to its native Gaelic again, was racing away.

I will ask Edinburgh to have those two men boiled in oil.

I hope he was not heading for the airport, but I wanted to know. Either way. They were to see him into the airport. Or past it.

And I will make Ritchie very sorry that he showed that photograph. An identity parade would achieve nothing now.

Why would Ritchie have a photograph of Calder? They know each other well. Did Ritchie show the photograph to the witness so that the identification of Calder would not stand up in court?

It was Ritchie who spoke to Edinburgh.

If I thought . . . But no. I would not act without proof. And I will not get proof now. I must watch Ritchie in future. Especially in any case which involves Calder.

These two men will not let anything slip. I must fire the big gun.

'There will be no bail on a murder charge,' he said. 'Do you deny that yesterday you killed a man?' He thought: *It is hard to read the expression on a swollen face, but I think that he is amazed. And yet she seemed so sure.*

Keith felt his stomach swoop down, and he clenched his buttocks in case it went all the way. *Nobody ever died of busted knee-caps. Or did they?* He turned towards Enterkin.

'Deny it,' the solicitor said.

'Certainly I deny it. Who's dead?'

'You're trying to tell me that you don't know?'

'I am telling you. I'm giving you my positive assurance that I've no bloody idea.'

'And you'd swear to that?'

'I'd put it to music and sing it.'

'I doubt the court would find it of great evidential value,' Munro said. He scratched his chin. 'I will put it to you straight,' he said suddenly. 'Keith Calder, do you deny that yesterday you killed your partner, Wallace James?'

Eleven

Keith's mouth was bone dry, and his stomach, which had ceased its churning, resumed its gyrations. He heard Enterkin gasp.

'Wallace is *dead?*' Keith said at last.

'Please record,' said Enterkin, 'that Mr Calder's tone was interrogatory.'

Through a haze of grief, Keith thought:

Wallace is dead? What do I tell Janet? How?

He must have met Warrender.

If if happened in Lewis, they wouldn't think I did it.

Between the Angus Hotel and Riverside Drive?

How can I drop Warrender in it, without dropping Mrs Heller and her little friends as well?

Mr Enterkin was asking, 'Has the body been identified positively as being that of Mr James?'

'I can't tell you that,' Munro said. Even through his bemusement, Keith recogised the evasive tone. He came alert.

'Then,' Enterkin said, 'my client is not saying another word. You can't seriously expect him to make any statement in the face of vague, unspecific and unsubstantiated allegations.'

'An honest man –' Munro began.

'The most honest man in the world,' Enterkin said firmly, 'yes, even a man as honest as my client, could talk himself into trouble if he let himself be drawn into that sort of trap. Do you, in fact, have a body?'

'Not as yet,' Munro admitted. 'The inshore lifeboat is doing a search of the Tay and the frogmen are out. But we do not need a body.'

'You do before you can come to court,' Enterkin said. 'God knows how many years it is since a Scottish court entertained a murder charge without a body.'

'We can prove death in other ways, and the circumstantial evidence is strong. Mr James left here yesterday to meet Mr Calder in Dundee. They had quarrelled because Mr Calder was using his time and the firm's money to build up his own collection of antique guns. Mrs James has not heard from her husband again, and Mr Calder is heading for Turnhouse Airport. To that, add Mr Calder's long infatuation with Mrs James... Hard evidence will follow, if he did this thing. Forensic evidence, such as bloodstains in the boot of his car.'

Keith, fortunately, was dumbstruck. There was a certain distorted truth in each of the points made. Except that he had never had an affair with Janet, only a five year flirtation that neither of them had ever taken seriously. As to forensic evidence in the boot of his car, Keith wished them joy. His car had been used to transport hares, rabbits and roe-deer, not to mention, at a rough count, eleven different quarry species of birds.

'Has Mrs James signed a statement?' Enterkin asked.

'She has indeed.'

'Accusing Mr Calder of murdering her husband?'

'Implying just that.'

Keith's mind came unstuck.

Why would Janet want to frame me? A woman scorned? I never scorned her, so's you'd notice.

Wal could have told her about the collection, but he'd never have called it a quarrel.

I told Wal I'd got my face bashed up. He'd have told Janet before he left. But why's she left the fuzz thinking that it happened in a fight with Wal?

There's something twisted here, something to do with that damned civil engineer, that builder of roads and sewers.

I've got to be all right.

Just so Wal comes back. But – St Bilda of Rhodes and Suez! – suppose he meets Warrender over in Lewis and ends up buried in the heather!

Molly knows he was o.k. after I got marked. The hotel staff know when I came in with lumps on my face. The pilot knows Wallace was all right at that time.

Better make sure they remember.

But why?

Somebody hates me? There's no point unless it'd stand up in court.

So what have I missed.

Look at it the other way round. Somebody gets something they wanted. So what have they got? Me, out of circulation? A red herring?

A red herring. Hold onto that thought. Nobody looking at Millmont House? Nobody looking at Wallace? Both.

Police pricking up their ears, sniffing with long, Hebridean noses. Sniffing around Millmont House. Mrs Heller starts worrying. What would I worry about in her shoes?

Yes, but what else?

Got it! If they're checking on us, the trail would lead through me . . . Wallace . . . Mrs Illingworth . . . Donald of that ilk . . . and right back to dead bodies at Millmont House. Give them a temporary explanation for Wal's absence and for my face and they don't look for him in Lewis. They look for him in the Tay, and by the time he turns up again the scent's cold.

So Mrs Heller has a quiet word with Janet. Crafty bitch!

And all I've got to do is to sit tight and pray to God that I've guessed it right. Otherwise I'm up to my ankles in clag, from head-first.

'I have nothing whatever to say.'

'Splendid!' Enterkin said. 'You heard my client, Chief Inspector. Now, if I can have a private confabulation with him, we'll see if we can't be a little more helpful.'

Chief Inspector Munro sighed the sigh of a man surrounded by unco-operative fools and knaves. 'Use this room,' he said. 'I'll get myself something to eat. And while I'm out of the room I'll be phoning Dundee. A car just like Mr Calder's was seen at Broughty Ferry Harbour, so they've got a diver down. I shall be wanting to hear what he's found.'

'A real diver?' Keith asked. 'Helmet and boots? Not just a frogman?'

'A real diver.'

'Give him my compliments,' Keith said, 'and remind him not to fart.' He hated to waste a joke.

Chief Inspector Munro slammed the door pettishly behind him.

Keith waited inside the black cavern of his head. Without seeing it he could visualise Mr Enterkin's expression because, when given food for thought, the solicitor would purse and protrude his lips as if giving the kiss of life to a dormouse. Keith forced one eyelid up a fraction. Yes. Just so.

'You'd better tell me all about it,' Enterkin said at last.

'When I said that I'd nothing to say, I meant to anybody.'

Enterkin grunted. 'Munro's just fishing for information,' he said. 'Throw him some tiddlers and he'll let you go. Otherwise, if I push it to get you out of here, he'll throw some kind of charge at you.'

'But as long as I'm here, just "helping with enquiries", nothing'll get into the press?'

'It shouldn't,' Enterkin said doubtfully.

'I like it here,' Keith said. 'You get Molly to pop me in my tape-recorder, and then get on up to Dundee and make sure that the hotel staff remember that my face was already banged up before Wallace got there. But don't lead Munro there. I don't want out of here just yet, and we can always add vexatious arrest to the other writs, when Wallace walks in unskaithed.'

'You're sure that he will walk in?'

'Sure beyond all reasonable doubt.'

'That should be good enough for one of my calling. And you're not saying anything until he does? I think you're quite right,' Enterkin said with quiet significance. 'Tell me this, though. Am I working for you or for Millmont House?'

'Good God!' Keith said. 'You're not supposed to know about Millmont House. You're a married man.'

'Recently married.'

'Before that, you told me that you had a "comfortable arrangement".'

Enterkin chuckled. 'And so I did,' he said. 'No arrangement is as comfortable as one that's bought and paid for.'

Keith paused for thought. Janet knew well who would be called to act as his solicitor. 'You know more than you're letting on, don't you?' he suggested.

'Just a little.'

'Well, keep Munro on the hop. Serve writs on him. Not *Habeus Corpus* –'

'*Habeus Corpus* doesn't run in Scotland.'

'Well, whatever our equivalent is, not that. Assault and defamation. But don't push him so hard that he'll bring charges.'

'You do understand,' Enterkin said slowly, 'that if it came to court and you wanted me to testify on oath, I'd have to say that I saw you fall down on purpose.'

'Yes, of course,' Keith said. 'But it won't go that far.'

'At this time,' Keith said into the microphone, 'when changes in warfare had made the once unbeatable Brown Bess musket obsolete, Captain Patrick Ferguson perfected a rifle, loaded through the breech by way of a threaded plug which screwed downward when the trigger-guard was turned. The ease and speed of reloading, and the range and accuracy deriving from the tight fit of the ball to the rifling, gave this weapon superiority even over its American rivals.

'However, Lord North's –'

Keith was interrupted in full flow of dictation by the arrival of Chief Inspector Munro in his cell. He fumbled for the recorder and switched it off.

'Is there anything that you've decided to tell me?' Munro's hissing Highland voice asked.

'You'll be glad to hear that the doctor does not expect any permanent ill-effects. On the other hand,' Keith said, 'I shall carry a scar for the rest of my days, which will count against you when we come to court. Did they find Wal's body in Broughty Ferry Harbour?'

'I think you know very well that they did not. The car that was seen there has been traced. It belonged to one of Thomson's sub-editors, doing his courting. I am becoming surer by the minute that you did not kill your partner, so why do you persist in wasting my time?'

'I'm not wasting it. You're wasting it. Tell me what law requires a man to clear himself of a charge that hasn't been brought if he doesn't want to.'

'Perhaps there is no law,' Munro said. 'I shall have to find out. But the only reason I ever knew for a man not to defend himself at all when he was innocent was because he had committed a different crime on that day. I have been looking over the reports of yesterday's crimes. I do not suppose that you robbed a bank in Kelvingrove, and as for a rape in Peterhead I would not put it past you but we got the man. In fact, once we eliminate housebreaking, we are left with the two men who were assaulted and left attached to a tree. That deed has your hallmark.'

'The man who is in hospital has stated that he has no intention of making a statement. But we now know his identity, and his usual companion is of the same description as the other victim. When we catch up with him, it may be that he will make a statement.'

Keith fingered his swollen face. *I wouldn't count on it*, he thought. *Sauce for the goose.* He said nothing.

'Your wife was more co-operative,' Munro went on. 'She allowed us to look in your car. Your gun had been fired.'

'I took a shot at a pigeon before I left.'

'And there was an empty cartridge in your pocket.'

'I pick up my cartridge-cases. Cattle can choke on them.'

'Is that how your partner died? It is all very interesting,' Munro said. 'I have just had a report. The man who is in hospital with the broken kneecap. There was shot embedded in the sole of one of his shoes. Number six, the same as your cartridge-case.'

'That might be meaningful except that my cartridges are reloads. The numbers printed on them don't mean a damn thing. And,' Keith added, 'if the silly sod makes a habit of fluttering out of the treetops he must expect to get shot at occasionally. He probably broke his kneecap when he crash-landed.'

'Very funny,' Munro said sadly. 'There are other ways a man could get shot into the sole of his shoe. For instance, somebody might have taken a shot at him while he was down on his face. Crawling away, perhaps, with a broken kneecap.'

'I wouldn't know,' Keith said. He picked up his microphone.

'Put that thing down,' Munro said irritably. 'You are not out of trouble by a long way. The one crime is not an alibi for the other. I don't think you killed your partner, but I think that you committed the most grievous of bodily harm on the man with the broken kneecap. If you are helpful about your movements for the rest of the day we just might not encourage either man to make a complaint. Well? Have you anything to say?'

'Quite a lot,' Keith said, 'but not on the subject you're wanting.' He groped for the switch and turned on his tape-recorder, and with the microphone in his hand he slid the button. '– corrupt and incompetent administration,' he said with relish, 'seeking only the greatest opportunities for personal reward –' he heard Munro flounce out of the cell and the click of the lock '–preferred to buy mercenaries from German princelings. Only a hundred Ferguson Rifles were ever made, and when Ferguson himself was killed at Kings Mountain the military project was dropped although Durs Egg continued to build commercial models.

'It has been said that there was no one cause of the loss of the War of Independence. That may be true. But, had the British Army been properly equipped, the American colonies might to this day . . .'

Keith paused and put down the microphone. Satisfactory wording eluded him. He wanted to add '. . . have been ours for the milking,' but his publisher was hoping for sales in the United States. He would ask Wallace. When Wallace came back.

Keith spent nearly three days in Newton Lauder's cells, helping the police with their enquiries in as unhelpful a manner as he could manage. His only talking was into the tape-recorder. The rough framework of his book took on shape.

The original contours of his face began to emerge. He could keep his eyes half-open for minutes at a time although, as he frequently pointed out, it was hardly worth the bother.

From time to time he laid the microphone aside and went again over his logic. Wallace's continued absence was worrying. He imagined Wal buried under the heather and Janet walking under a bus or running off with the milkman. His, Keith's, position would be awkward, to say the least. But if ever he doubted his logic, Molly's manner, whenever she came to visit, reassured him. Molly, although she tried to hide it, was highly amused, and she acted so like a Victorian heroine visiting the condemned cell that even the humourless Munro was caught smiling. Keith would have demanded an explanation; but he admitted to himself that if he had been in Munro's shoes the visiting room would have been dotted with listening devices.

By the evening of the second day Molly's act was becoming strained, and Keith was worried.

Twelve

Late in the morning of the third day, Keith was turned loose. He was given neither explanation nor information, and the officers present seemed to be avoiding his eye. He was offered a lift home, but declined it. The action would not be at Briesland House.

He crossed the square. His car was parked, crookedly, near the shop.

In the shop Minnie Pilrig, the maiden lady who helped out in times of stress, was coping single-handed with a rush of four customers. She raised her eyes from Keith to the ceiling. Correctly interpreting the glance, Keith ducked out of the shop door and in at the next, and climbed the stair to the flat where he and Molly had started their married life. Here he found his wife and daughter, the two dogs and Janet, all listening raptly to the wanderer returned.

Keith's arrival seemed to be amusing.

'Here comes the gaol-bird,' said Janet.

'I asked them if they'd keep you another year or two,' Molly told him, 'but they said they couldn't afford to, the way you eat.'

Keith stooped and patted the dogs, fawning around his feet. 'That's all very well,' he told Wallace. 'I guessed that the whole thing was a put-up job to keep Munro off your trail. But what the hell kept you? I suppose you've been living it up in some plush hotel while I was eating dried camel-dung and sleeping on concrete?'

'As a matter of fact,' Wallace said, 'I was. Have you eaten?'

'Yes. They feed you early in the nick.'

'I wouldn't know about that. I'll tell you my tale in the car. No point boring the girls with it again, and we'd better see Mrs Heller as soon as possible.'

'You got something, then?'

'Come on.' Wallace almost dragged him out of the flat and down to the street. 'Which car shall we take?'

'Yours,' Keith said. 'I intend to get stoned out of my mind. I think I've earned it.'

128

As soon as Wallace had the car in motion, Keith said 'Well?'

'Very.'

'I suppose you realise that I was shitting bricks in there, in case you met up with Warrender and never came back and nobody believed Janet. Did you bump into Warrender, by the way? You don't look marked.'

'I'm not. I was a couple of days ahead of him, and I told you that I use my head. The chopper was picking me up at Millmont House anyway. Debbie Heller dug out a letter from Humbert Brown and we Xeroxed the letterhead and typed up an authentic-looking letter to Warrender, telling him to get the hell up to Lerwick where a man answering Don Donaldson's description had been making enquiries about holiday accommodation on a remote croft. We added that the police were sniffing along his trail, so he'd better use another name.'

'It could take him months to search the Shetlands,' Keith said. 'All those islands.'

'That's what we thought. So last thing when the chopper pilot dropped me, I told him to leave the letter at Stornaway Airport for Mr Warrender, and ask them to announce its existence over the loudspeakers every time passengers came in from the mainland. I gave him twenty quid to back it up with. And I'd asked Debbie to phone the harbours at Stornaway and Tarbert, just in case he crossed by ferry, and promise a reward if they'd approach every passenger with a bruised face and pass on a message to Warrender that the letter was waiting at the airport for him. I checked up yesterday, and the letter was uplifted. They said he'd gone back on the next plane. But I warned Illingworth's mother not to trust him, just in case.'

'You found her, then?'

'I found her. When the chopper took me over we could see one or two faint lights around Bernera, but the brightest group was what seemed to be an hotel on the mainland of Lewis, not very far away. So I had the pilot put me down on the beach near there and I walked up. Sure enough, it was an hotel and the night porter gave me a room. He was waiting up for a fishing-party.

'After breakfast I found a woman behind the desk. She was a

hard-faced old bag but done up to kill in satin and high heels. So I asked her where I might find the Mrs Illingworth who used to live in Dundee.

'She gave me a look like a basilisk with a slipped disc. "I'm Mrs Illingworth," she said. "What the hell can I do for you?" Not in so many words, of course.

'Well, that caught me flat-footed and I got a bad case of the stutters, so I excused myself and went for a couple of stiff drinks. They alter the clock to suit the licensing hours over there. I gathered from the barmaid – a very gorgeous barmaid in that tall, big-boned Highland style – that Mrs Illingworth owned the place. It had been her family's ancestral home, and she's spent the past years working it up into a sporting hotel. There's some nice old guns on the walls – her husband's, I suppose.

'When I felt a bit stronger, I went back and tackled her.'

'With all the aggression of a cornered bathmat?' Keith suggested.

'Probably. You see, I wanted to know something but I hadn't the faintest idea what I wanted to find out. Anyway, I bought her coffee in the lounge. I said that I knew her son, and I was worried because he seemed to have gone off in a hurry and somebody seemed to be trying to set him up in his absence. I kept it vague but ominous. She loosened up a bit. Not much of a bit, but a bit. Over the next day or so, I dug out of her that Harold Fosdyke, or somebody who sounded like his twin, had been around about a month before, asking veiled questions about young Donald. He introduced himself as Henry Foster, a friend of Donald's child-hood in Dundee, and she said that she did remember him from those days because he'd been fat then and he was fat still. So Foster's probably his real name. But what if anything he'd found out she couldn't think. There'd been nobody else. Young Donald hadn't contacted her. He never did, although she wrote to him from time to time.

'Well, we weren't getting any forwarder. Foster had been over, snooping. Presumably he'd dug up something. But what the hell? And what had given Warrender the idea that there was anything to be learned in Lewis?

'I had one thing going for me with the old biddy. Along with

130

the house and some fishing rights and a place where some geese come in the autumn, she'd inherited a big stretch of hill and moorland. It had been hung up in a dispute with the Crofting Commission, but now it's all free and clear and she wanted to know whether she could do anything with it. Like stalking and grouse.

'Well, I don't know a damn thing about stalking. I said Ronnie'd go over later and advise her.'

'You don't know a damn thing about grouse either,' Keith said.

'I know enough, and I went out to look at it. There were a few starved-looking grouse, and mile upon mile of ancient heather. Most of the ground sloped away from the prevailing wind, so I thought she was in with a chance. She'd been asking about rearing grouse and I explained that you couldn't and didn't need to. I told her about heather-burning and grit. I also told her about predator control and she said that she knew just the man.

'Suddenly we were buddies, and she invited me into her private rooms for coffee. And as soon as I walked in I saw what Foster, if that's his real name, must have seen. This is the bit that I didn't tell Janet and Molly.'

'You didn't tell me either,' Keith said. 'Come to the point.'

Without taking his eyes off the road, Wallace took a photograph, framed in leather, out of his inside pocket. 'I don't suppose she'll notice it's gone. She had a thousand like it, but only one of her.'

Keith studied the photograph, puzzled. 'I don't get it,' he said.

'Imagine her with fair hair.'

Keith called upon the sacred arsehole of St Bilda, the second from the left. 'So *that's* why she fancied the guns on her wall,' he added. 'Childhood memories.'

Mrs Heller's reaction was framed less imaginatively. 'That's the wickedest thing I've ever come across,' she said.

'What is?' Keith asked carefully.

'I've known men come here for a variety of wacky reasons, but this is the first time a man hated his family so much that he'd come here and pay to screw his own sister.'

'Yes, I thought we might be at cross-purposes. I think you're looking at it upside down,' Keith said.

'It explains why he might kill the man who found out.'

'It doesn't explain why he'd take a boyhood friend along with him, if he didn't want him to know. Look at it this way up. Illingworth had lost touch with his family. He got an occasional letter from his mother, but never replied. He wouldn't recognise his own sister, not with fair hair; she'd have been a child when the family split up. Then a boyhood acquaintance who had something to gain from getting Illingworth under his thumb goes over to Lewis to see what he can find out. And the luck's running his way. He sees a photograph of Illingworth's sister, and recognises her as a high-class –'

'Tart,' said Mrs Heller.

'Thank you. Foster's got what he wants. He looks up Illingworth, renews old friendship if that's what it was. There's no secret about Illingworth's mode of life. It wouldn't be difficult to tempt Illingworth into making a date for a visit here and then to book a particular girl for him.'

'His sister? So that he could be blackmailed?' For the first time, Mrs Heller sounded truly shocked. 'I was right. That really is the lousiest trick I've ever heard of. But don't rush ahead too fast. We haven't established a motive. Humbert Brown have shown an interest, but we've no evidence of a connection between them and Foster.'

'We're assuming Humbert Brown,' Keith said. 'Do they have a motive for getting Donald Illingworth under their thumb?'

'By God they do!' Wallace said.

'Then phone them,' Keith told Mrs Heller. 'Ask to speak to Henry Foster on urgent business. See what they say.'

She shrugged. 'It's worth a try,' she said. She used her intercom to tell the duty porter to place the call and then sat with her fingers drumming on the handset. 'So,' she said. 'As we see it, Foster wanted a hold over Illingworth and found out that Hilary was his sister. He realised that the two of them wouldn't recognise each other. So he brought him here, encouraged him to drink himself stupid and blow some pot as well, and threw him at her. Then he tried to apply the pressure. It was too much for Illingworth, who killed him and is now hanging about abroad, waiting to see what

132

happens. Is that about the size of it?'

'That's about it,' Keith said. 'There's room for variation here or there, but it's a good enough working hypothesis for the moment.'

She scowled, making a travesty of her usually lovely face. 'I don't like it. I'll tell you –' The respectful buzz of the intercom broke in. She picked up the handset and listened in silence for a few seconds. 'Tell her no.' She slammed down the handset and looked from Keith to Wallace and back again. 'The telephone girl at Humbert Brown regrets that Mr Foster has been off work for the past week, presumed sick, and would anybody else do?'

'It fits together,' Keith said. 'And I bet that what you don't like is what I don't like.'

'I don't like it either,' Wallace said.

'What?' Keith and Mrs Heller said together.

'Illingworth wouldn't cave in, or get into enough of a tizzy to kill somebody, just at a threat that Foster would go around telling everybody that he'd committed incest, or even that his sister was a tart. Hilary would hardly confirm the story. It'd be actionable. He'd need good solid proof, or Illingworth would have told him to go to hell.'

Keith nodded.

'That's what I was afraid of,' Debbie Heller said. 'We're not stupid, and neither was Foster. Those chalets are designed to be proof against Peeping Toms. I can't see Foster lurking about outside with a camera, hoping they'd leave the door open; and Annette said that he'd given her a pretty thorough servicing, which would have been just at the time for proof-getting.' Her voice fell silent.

'Go on,' Keith said. 'It's for you to say aloud.'

'I'm afraid so. All right. In his shoes, I'd bribe one of the porters.'

'To make a tape off the video system?'

'Exactly. Damn!' she said suddenly. 'I can take almost anything else, but this ... Any one of them could do it, because that's what we did for the police last year when they wanted evidence about conspiracy over a bank fraud and the men had been meeting here. All he'd have to do would be to borrow the video machine out of an unoccupied chalet, put it under the desk, plug it in, and set the time-clock if he was called away. The machines are only there for viewing blue films on, but the recording part of them still works.'

'It would have to be the duty porter,' Wallace said. 'That makes it Bert. I'd put him down as trustworthy.'

Mrs Heller's grunt was unladylike. 'So would I,' she said. 'But having Donald Illingworth in their pocket could be worth a million or upward to Humbert Brown. They could well afford to lay out a thousand or two. Bert wouldn't be proof against that sort of inducement.'

'Not many would.'

Wallace moved uneasily in his seat. 'Assuming that there was a video-t-tape,' he said, 'Foster would've collected it before he started making any threats. In that case, Illingworth would have taken it off him. So it's probably at the bottom of Funchal Bay.'

'B-but, just as you said, Debbie, Foster wasn't stupid. He'd know that when you corrupt a man for a thousand or two he starts wondering where the next ten grand's coming from. It would be only too easy for Bert to record any discussions in either chalet. The fact that Foster got killed suggests that he'd had his confrontation with Illingworth. Why would he do that here, when he could have waited until they were in the car to go home, or even some time next month?'

'He may have asked him to come out for a stroll, or to sit in the car while they talked,' Mrs Heller said.

'Unless,' Keith said, 'he needed something extra, to hold over Illingworth or to convince his employers that he'd done his job. After all, they'd only have a bum and a couple of faces to go by. If I was ever bastard enough to pull a stunt like that, I'd make the deal include the second tape, to be handed over to me.'

'Jesus wept!' Debbie Heller said slowly. 'If a second tape ever existed, it all depends on whether Foster collected it. If he did, he'd have put it with the other one and Illingworth would have taken them both. If not, the odds are that Bert's still got it. A bit of jam for the fuzz if they can find it.'

'The fuzz?' Keith lost the thread of discussion for a moment.

'You've convinced me all over again. We know all we need to know. There was a murder committed here. We know who by. We know the motive. We've got enough evidence to cut short any investigation. We've got no option but to call the police. And you're going to say "I told you so",' she added bitterly. 'Well, you've earned your fee, so I suppose you've earned that too.'

'I did tell you so, but that isn't what I was going to say. You've swung round in your attitude, and I've swung round in mine.

'Never mind where our financial interests lie, let's look at this thing in the abstract. We've got a classic dilemma. A campaigner for good was deliberately manoeuvred into a position in which he can be shown to have gone to a brothel and shagged his own sister, and we presume that he was being blackmailed into throwing his weight on the side which he believed to be evil. All this when he had set out to do no more than be about as promiscuous as three-quarters of the human race. And, at the time, he was full of booze and pot. So he shoots the bugger. In his place I'd probably have done much the same.

'We've got a case which could probably be proved in court, given the extra evidence that the police might dig up. Illingworth might get off, he might be convicted – either way he'd be ruined. And it wouldn't do any of us any good.

'Nobody knows much about this except ourselves, and we may decide that we can deal with any dangers.

'That, I suggest, leaves the ball in our court, rather than in any other kind of court. The law wouldn't agree, but then, the law and justice don't always meet in the middle.

'You can go along with me or not, just as you wish. I'm pointing out to you that Foster's dead anyway and nothing can change that. Illingworth is still around, and still has a lot of potential to do good. I'm not only thinking about the corruption; we've seen some of the violence and blackmail that can follow in corruption's wake.

'It's wrong to take no action out of inertia. But what I'm suggesting to you is that this is one case in which it would be right to take a positive decision to take no action, and that's a very different thing.'

Debbie Heller got up, walked to the window and stood looking out. The sunlight etched every soft curve of her figure through her thin dress. She might as well have been naked, and Keith thought that she knew it. He guessed that it gave her some comfort in a time of stress to be seen as a woman.

'You're right,' she said at last. 'And I'm not saying that out of self-interest. Sometimes justice is more important than law. But Donald Illingworth will have to go along with us.'

'I'm sure,' Keith said carefully, 'that you have no intention of putting pressure on him in your turn.' He tried to keep any questioning note out of his voice.

Without turning round she shook her head impatiently so that the red-gold locks flickered like flame in the sunlight. 'We don't play that some of game,' she said. 'If we lost our reputation for being above blackmail we'd lose all our customers the same day. And while we're turning over the sort of money that we are, we'd have to be out of our tiny minds. Illingworth has to go along because there's no point in our taking one hell of a risk if he's going to lose his nerve and top himself, or run to the cops and confess. That'd just land us all in it. Somebody must go out and see him, convice him that it's all over and that he's got to get back on the ball.'

'Not me,' Keith said quickly.

'I'd b-be no good,' Wallace said. 'The one thing I'm no good at is persuading hostile strangers. Keith's bloody good at that.'

'Send one of the girls. Send ten of them.'

'He doesn't trust women,' Debbie Heller said over her shoulder. 'You're elected.'

Keith, who had only flown once in his life and that on a back-up aircraft on a short hop to Inverness, had an immediate vision of being lifted to the upmost stretch of vertigo in an aircraft built out of wet cardboard. He uttered a faint, negative croak.

Mrs Heller resumed her seat and became again the Chairman of the Group. 'Get this straight,' she said. 'You've earned your fee, and you'll get it. But if Illingworth won't play ball we can't take a chance on covering this up. So there could still be a scandal, and we needn't have bothered hiring you to do an investigation for us. You'll have to find another lender, and it'd cost you a damn sight more than your fee. And you'll get no bonus, and I personally will take that Ferguson popgun and chop it up for firewood.

'On the other hand, if you do this for me and we can settle the whole thing without any scandal, you'll get your bonus and your old gun.' She eyed Keith in careful calculation. She was expert at judging a price. 'And I'll throw in something else. You can have any two other guns off that wall. Or how about the services of one or two of the girls for a night? I've already pledged enough of the group's money to you.'

Keith's fear of flying began to recede in favour of a long-standing fantasy. 'How about,' he counted silently, 'six of your girls?'

'All at the same time?' She did not seem at all surprised.

'Yes.'

She leaned forward and activated the computer terminal on the desk. 'Nine-thirty Thursday,' she suggested. 'Make up your mind about Madeira. If you're on, you'd better slip out to the porter's desk and ask him to book you out and back through the travel agents. Phone your wife from the desk and ask her if she'd like a week in Madeira, all expenses paid by your client. Then come back in here and we'll have a few words about how to keep Humbert Brown in line.'

Keith got to his feet and walked very slowly to the door. In the doorway, he came to a complete halt. 'Make it a very few words,' he said. 'I want Wal to get me out of here before I change my mind. I'll take the guns.' He closed the door behind him gently, as if on a favourite dream.

'Poor Keith,' Wallace said. 'Flying scares him rigid.'

'He won't like Madeira, then.' Mrs Heller chuckled suddenly. 'The main runway looks like somebody's garden path, fallen off a cliff. I went there once with a boy-friend.'

'Me,' said Wallace.

She looked at him in surprise. 'So it was! And we spent the fort-night working-out the constitution and financial structure of Personal Service.'

'Not all the time,' Wallace said.

'No, not all the time. Those were good days, Wal.'

'They were.'

The two smiled at each other in comfortable nostalgia.

Thirteen

Keith, as a rule, was self-reliant to a degree which distressed his wife. Molly would have enjoyed being depended upon from time to time. Yet there was one errand which neither of them fancied, and Keith had held out the Madeira trip as bribe. As she walked down the middle of the long hospital ward she wondered whether a few days in tropical luxury would be an adequate recompense.

Jim Bardolph was in an end bed, staring morosely out of the window at a cloudy sky. His belly was a mound under the bed-clothes, dwarfed by his leg raised in the traction harness. He looked round as Molly took the chair beside his bed, and there was an appreciative twist to his swollen mouth. Molly was an attractive woman when she took the trouble, and she had taken the trouble today.

'Hullo,' she said, more brightly than she felt. 'How are you mending?'

'No' so bad. Are you yin o' they socialist workers?'

'Not me. When do you think they'll let you go home to Possilpark?' Keith had been doing some investigating on his own account.

'Twa weeks yet. I don't know you. Just who are you?'

'I'm Molly Calder. You know. You tried to –'

'Whit! That –'

She hushed him quickly and his voice trailed away. 'Shout if you want,' she said. 'I can walk out of here any time I like. You've got to stay here and live with it.'

Bardolph glowered, but he lowered his voice to a ferocious whisper. 'Yon bogger! I'll clour him. Just you tell him from me that as soon as I can walk right I'll come and tear his gut out and tie –' A new thought broke the flow of his rhetoric. 'Hey! Whit d'ye ken about Possilpark?'

'You live in Ravensrigg Crescent,' Molly said quietly. 'With Jeannie and the three kids. Keith said that if you ever set foot in

138

Newton Lauder again he'll burn Ravensrigg Crescent from end to end with them in it, before you've even got the length of the Square.'

Bardolph was squinting with emotion. He struggled to get up on his elbows. 'An' you tell that cunt – beggin' your pardon – that if he comes near Possilpark . . . if he . . .' Bardolph fell silent and lay back on the pillow.

'He won't if you don't. Remember, it was you who started all this.'

'Me? Whit way was it me?' Bardolph demanded.

'You threatened Keith that you'd harm me and Deborah.'

'I didn't mean it,' Bardolph said plaintively. 'It's just one of the things you say.'

'Well, you'd better not go on saying it. The last person who harmed me, Keith killed him,' Molly said, not without a touch of quiet pride.

'And he got off?' Bardolph sounded respectful.

'They couldn't touch him. Keith put a scare into him and then chased him across the moors until the man dropped with a heart attack. But the point is, you'd have done the same yourself if somebody threatened Jeannie or the weans.'

'But it wisna' me did it. It's me lying here and not a penny coming in.'

'That's what I came to tell you about,' Molly said. 'Keith's fixed it that if you don't make any trouble but help us deal with your mate Warrender, you'll get paid by the day until you can work again.'

'Including weekends?'

'Well . . .'

'I'm in here weekends,' Bardolph pointed out reasonably.

'I'll see if we can fix it.'

'That's great. Sundays are double time. You get a message to Cyril to come and see me, and I'll call him off. Sooner the better. Folk think I'm hard, but he's the hard man. And your Keith blacked his eye for him.'

'Both of them,' Molly said. 'But he did the same to Keith.'

'Where's Cyril now?' he asked.

Molly told him of Warrender's travels in the Shetland Isles, and

Bardolph shook with laughter until his knee pained him back into seriousness. 'Youse just leave Cyril to me,' he said. 'Just so's he gets paid up to when I tell him it's over, he'll be satisfied. Can you reach him and tell him to come and see me urgent?'

'We can reach him,' Molly said. 'The Shetlands are several islands and you can't move around far without crossing a ferry. A promise to the ferrymen of twenty quid to the man who tells him to phone a number ought to do it.' She pulled a well-wrapped parcel out of her shopping-bag and transferred it to the locker. 'Keith sent you a bottle. I was only to give it to you, to help your knee mend, if you were going to be . . . reasonable. It's a very special whisky. I'll have to be going now.'

'Aw!' Bardolph's face began to droop again.

Molly was filled with fresh compassion. 'Will you be out by the 23rd?' she asked.

His brow creased in calculation. 'Aye. Likely.'

'We're going abroad on holiday tomorrow. But Keith had tickets for the Billy Connolly concert at the Kelvin Hall. Would you like them?'

'The Big Yin? That'd be great! You're . . .' Bardolph paused, searched for the *mot juste* and found it. 'You're a wee smasher,' he said.

Fourteen

In a luxurious but impersonal bedroom high above the Bay of Funchal, Keith was locked in argument, albeit one-sided argument, with Donald Illingworth. The man was as lean and dark as his pictured image, but photographs could not show his manner. And this puzzled Keith. Illingworth's cast of feature, his description and occasional glimpses of a buried self all spoke of a quivering intensity; but all this was smothered under a blanket which Keith could not penetrate. It might have been residual shock, or a restraint imposed by his own will for some unguessable reason. And he looked older than his photographs. Despite his week on the island, his skin was still white.

'I don't think you've listened to a bloody word I've uttered,' Keith said at last.

'I've listened,' Illingworth said woodenly.

'No, you haven't. You've heard but not listened. Now ...' Keith had brought his bottle of duty-free with him and a spare glass. He opened the bottle and started pouring. 'Now we're going to have a dram to loosen you up and I'll see if I can get through to you.'

Illingworth shivered. 'I'm not taking any drink. If I hadn't been stoned to hell and gone none of this would have happened.'

'Yes it *would*,' Keith said irritably. 'That's what I've been trying to get over to you. You were deliberately set up. You went there expecting a certain kind of a party, and you'd have been trapped even if you'd been stone cold sober. Now I don't want to get you fu', and if you'll only take in what I'm saying there'll be no need, but you've been sitting here for a week in a nervous dither, not even going out into the sunshine, waiting and wondering whether they were coming after you, and you're wound up as tight as a gnat's twat. Then, suddenly, somebody walks in out of the blue with the whole story laid bare, and your mind's slammed shut. Instead of listening to my pearls of wisdom, you're wondering whether to do something drastic to yourself.'

141

For the first time, Illingworth showed a flicker of expression. Keith thought that it was almost a smile. 'I'm not, you know. I've already made up my mind and you can't stop me. Even when I thought that I might get away with it, I knew that I wouldn't be able to live with myself. I only went to the Game Fair because I had a bet on with three club-members and I couldn't think of an excuse that wouldn't land me in more damned lies. Then I saw your wife taking photographs. She mightn't have seen me, so I pinched her bag of films. She got them back all right?'

'Yes.'

'That's good. When I opened the bag and saw that the films were unexposed, I knew I was done for. I'd booked my holiday so I came out anyway, but the more I've thought about it the more hopeless it all seems. So all I'm puzzling out now is how to do it with the least bother to everybody else.'

'Then you may as well have a dram to give you the courage.'

Illingworth picked up his glass, added water, made a sketchy salute and then drank. 'Go on,' he said. 'But you can't change black into white. Facts are facts.'

'Facts are never facts, and sometime you can turn black into white just by switching the light on.' Surreptitiously, Keith topped up the other's glass. Now that Illingworth was answering in more than monosyllables he felt that he might begin to break through the barrier. Perhaps what Molly had called his homespun philosophy might produce the mood that would accept practical arguments. 'Colours change, the way you look at them. You were deliberately trapped. You chose a certain way out. It might have been better not to, but in similar circumstances I could have done the same.'

Illingworth drank again. 'The fact of the matter is, I . . . had sex with my prostitute sister and killed a man to shut his mouth about it. Dress the fact up how you like, that's the way I see it and that's the way the police and the papers and the world – and my mother – will see it. But they don't prosecute the dead. If I'd rather be out of the way, to save myself the misery and others the scandal, why the hell should you care?'

'That's *good*,' Keith said. As he spoke, he realised that he was using the tone that he would have used to a pup in training. 'Now that you're asking questions, you're obliged to listen to me. All right, so you bedded your sister. You didn't know it at the time *and* you were being set up – those two facts alone should let your tender conscience off the hook. But you still have the willies because you're hung up on the shibboleths of a church that you lost faith in and abandoned years ago; and that church was acting as the mouthpiece of an establishment that changed its mind long since. Think about it dispassionately for a minute. Fornication became taboo because of two consequences – babies and the clap. Medical science has reduced those risks. The church still preaches morality because it has moved from being a practical necessity to being an abstract virtue. What's bugging you is that the word incest still has sinister, almost mystical overtones. But, for Christ's sake, the Egyptian Pharoahs usually married their own sisters, and it was only when it became obvious that inbreeding was bad for the stock that incest became banned. There was never any other reason. Since there was no intention of breeding, the incident doesn't matter a tinky's curse unless you torture yourself over it.'

Illingworth seemed to have slumped into his apathy again, except that he was watching Keith from under drooping eyelids. Now he stirred. 'How would you feel,' he demanded, 'if your sister turned out to be a tart?'

Keith cogitated, and while he thought he poured again. He had some reason to believe that a lady who was probably his half-sister on the wrong side of the blanket had practised for some years as a very successful tart. He had never before had to verbalise his thoughts on the matter, and he was surprised to find how clearcut they had become over the years. 'If I thought that circumstances had forced her into it,' he said, 'It'd break my heart. But if she made her own decision, I hope I'd be broadminded enough to go along. Every woman has a high chance of being dependant on a man, or men, or mankind generally for some part of their lives. It wasn't my idea, Nature planned it that way. Some of them commercialise the arrangement. But are they any worse than a woman who marries for money and then makes her husband miserable? At least a tart gives value for money. Or I expect she does, I wouldn't know. But don't forget that your sister made it to the top in a highly competitive market.'

143

Illingworth was giving Keith his full attention at last. 'You're a cynical sod.'

'I don't mean to be,' Keith said. The discussion was revealing him to himself. 'Instead of being stuffed with superstition I was left to draw my own conclusions. Next, you say you killed a man. True enough. That man had been if not your childhood friend at least a lifelong acquaintance, and he set out to trap you into doing what you did so that he could blackmail you into breaking your most deeply-held principles and letting his corruption go unchecked. I've heard of some evil deeds in my time. Perhaps I've committed a few, though I hope not. But I swear that's the foulest trick I ever heard of. I wouldn't say that he got much worse than he deserved. And, to make you vulnerable, he'd primed you with booze and pot. That was one hell of a mistake, because many men get more violent in that state. It seems to me that he was inviting exactly what he got. Given the circumstances, I think most men would have done something violent. But did you have to shoot him?'

'I wasn't going to,' Illingworth said. 'But I'm smaller than you and not a fighter. It came back to me that when we were young he could outfight me every time. So I walked in on him with the pistol and pointed it at him and told him to give me the video-tape. He was lying back in the easy chair, grinning at me. He wouldn't give up the tape. He patted his pocket, and I remember his exact words. He said, "If you think you can shoot me with that, go ahead. Otherwise, fuck off back to your sister. She's probably ready again by now",' Illingworth put his head down in his hands.

'So you shot him,' Keith said thoughtfully. 'I don't think I'd have done that, but there'd have been a fight that'd probably have killed him anyway. Right or wrong, you took the action that seemed right at the time. Now put it behind you and get on with your life. You've things to do. For God's sake, you're luckier than most of us. You've got a mission.'

Donald Illingworth's face, when he raised it again, was twisted between hope and despair. 'How can I?' His voice was choked and his lips were trembling. 'A man died. There's a widow. There'll be the police poking their noses. If you tracked it to me, so can they. Humbert Brown must have known what he was after. They

144

probably went to the police as soon as he went missing.'

Keith almost laughed. He thought that the worst was over. 'I'll tell you what steps have been taken,' he said. 'First off, you no longer have a tart for your sister. Mrs Heller did some digging. It seems that Hilary only went on the game to get out from under your mother's domination. That's a motive you'll sympathise with. Her ambition is to have her own disco-nightclub. Yes, I know, it sounds like hell to me too, but that's what she's set her heart on. And Debbie Heller says that although she's solid cotton-wool between the ears she's got enough savvy and sense of style and enough ruthless determination to make a go of it. You don't mind my talking about your sister that way?'

'Why not? It's just the way I remember her.'

'So Personal Service is launching one in Cardiff. It's far enough away that she shouldn't meet any old acquaintances. She goes in as manager under instruction for a year, and if she's got the flair it's all hers for her share in the company, on condition that she keeps her mouth tight shut.'

'She'd do that anyway.'

'I expect so. And she holds Mrs Heller in quite enough awe to make sure of it.

'Next, the body had to be disposed of more permanently. Your burial was a bit of a spur-of-the-moment. Frankly, the first fox to pass that way could have uncovered it. Couldn't you find a spade?'

'I got one out of a shed,' Illingworth said. 'But I hit rock before I was down two feet. I couldn't stay there all night digging holes.'

'Nor you could,' Keith said. 'Then, certain mouths had to be shut tight. It's been done, but I'm not saying how. You'll just have to take my word.'

'But who's going to shut the shutter's mouth?' Illingworth asked bitterly. 'I'm still wide open to blackmail. What does Personal Service want of me?'

'Bugger-all. I'll tell you something. Mrs Heller and her establishment have been an absolute total bloody revelation to me. You think of prostitution as being all mixed up with crime and violence and blackmail and God knows what-all. Debbie Heller's tough enough for any of that. But she's a top-class businesswoman, and she knows which side the bread's buttered. Outside of the – er – carnal side of things, the place is as strictly run as a finishing school, with a higher moral code than most reputable businesses. They only want you to pick up the threads again and fight the good fight. Stand for office in local government again if you like. Personal Service'll put no pressures on you, but if you need any help or backing . . .'

'Backing? From a knocking-shop?'

'It isn't a knocking-shop, it's a respectable group of companies,' Keith said. The words as he spoke them reminded him of something or somebody, but he hurried on. 'Take my advice, for what it's worth. Grab hold of any support you can get; other politicians all do. Personal Service with its big business hat on can swing a lot of weight. Use it to go places. Put the past behind you. You won't forget, of course. One never forgets one's mistakes, and a damn good thing too! But put guilt aside. It'll fade with time. Go back to your life. It's a good life, a life that most men would envy. A bit of shooting, a bit of crusading, a profession, and some women. Too damn many women, if you ask me.

For the first time, Illingworth had a spark in his eye. 'You're hardly the man to say that,' he pointed out. 'I mind the time men locked up their daughters when you were in Dundee.'

'I'm a happily married man now,' Keith said weakly.

'I think you're a happily married man who's jealous of somebody who can still screw around.'

Keith forced himself to sit silent. Remembering his itinerant, amorous youth and the self-satisfaction which he had felt on triumphing over a very real temptation at Millmont House, he supposed that there might be a grain of truth in the accusation. It was enough that Illingworth's nervous energy was at last being turned outward into the world and not into the dark recesses of his soul.

'Are you absolutely sure,' Illingworth asked, 'that nobody's going to talk?'

'Take my word for it,' Keith said again. He felt his guts loosen as he thought about it. He had been a hard man in his time, but that day he had been out of his class. And he had known it.

Howarth, of Humbert Brown (Contractors) Limited, had arrived

146

at Millmont House in a hostile mood barely suppressed. He came in a firm's Daimler of current year, and left some of the firm's rubber on the tarmac as he swung the car angrily round with headlamps blazing.

Keith and Debbie Heller were together to meet him in her office. He was a short, square man with iron-grey hair and a disciplined moustache of darker grey. His clothes were expensive and precise, and he brought with him an air of big business capability. Whatever the problem, it had better not dare to be insoluble. While he was still shaking hands he was already grumbling. 'Can't think what you want to see me about, alone and at this ungodly hour of the morning.' His voice was meant to be commanding, but was spoiled by a hesitant, peevish note in it.

'You'll see as we go along,' Mrs Heller said.

'Are we talking about the Firth Bay project?'

She sat down behind her desk and waved the two men into chairs. 'Not until this is settled,' she said. 'Probably not then, it all depends.'

'If you're talking about those two yobbos who you say attacked Mr Calder here, I can assure you –'

'We're talking about the late Henry Foster.'

There was a silence charged with the pain of dying hopes. 'Who?' Mr Howarth said, too late. 'Never heard of him.' Keith thought that he could almost hear the man's blood draining down from his head.

'That's funny,' Mrs Heller said. 'Your telephone girl had heard of him. She said that he was off sick, which is one way of putting it I suppose.' Howarth's face, which was ruddy in the best of times, was scarlet. Mrs Heller rode smoothly over his attempts to break into her discourse. 'Now, before you start to tell me that you do have a Henry Foster and he's off work with ringworm and you hire somebody to tell me that he's your Henry Foster, let me warn you not to say anything that you can't prove up to the hilt. Because I'm not accepting any stories without treble-checking them. So now is the time for you to make up your mind and commit yourself one way or the other. Do you want me as an ally or as an implacable enemy?'

Peering inquiringly through her horn-rimmed glasses, Debbie

Heller looked singularly unintimidating to Keith, but Howarth was taking her very seriously. 'I want you as an ally, of course,' he said.

'We shall see. We've got to the bottom of Foster's disappearance. And I've made quite sure that nobody on my staff will talk. You can believe me.'

'I do.' Howarth found a smile and produced it, carefully. 'You have a reputation for being able to make your staff jump through hoops.'

'Hold onto that thought. You may want it again later. We found out, and can prove, that Foster picked up what he considered to be some useful information about Donald Illingworth, namely that Illingworth's sister was one of the girls who use the chalets here.'

'Oh.'

'Yes. Now, it doesn't really matter a toss whether Foster was acting under direct instructions or was trying to get himself out of trouble with your firm by producing something which he knew would delight you, the fact is that he committed himself as your agent in pulling off one of the dirtiest frame-ups in history. And I'm not exaggerating. He contacted Illingworth, reminded him of a boyhood friendship and enticed him here. Foster made the bookings, and he was quite specific that he was booking the sister for the brother. The two hadn't seen each other since she was a child and she's changed the colour of her hair since then. The chance that they would recognise each other was infinitesimal. And he bribed one of my porters to make a visual recording of the resulting sex-act. Tell me, Mr Howarth, does that go to the top of your firm's list of dirty tricks, or is that fairly run-of-the-mill for you?'

Howarth leaned back in his chair and lit a cigarette. 'I knew nothing of this,' he said, 'nor did the firm. If Foster did as you say, he was acting on his own in the hope of a reward – which, incidentally, he would not have received if we had known anything of his methods. But can you prove any of this?'

'Without the least difficulty. The pressure that Foster put on him drove Illingworth so far off the balance of his mind that he killed Foster, and the original tape is no doubt destroyed. But my porter

148

also taped the confrontation between Foster and Illingworth when the threats were made. My porter says that Foster told him to make the second tape for your benefit, but I suspect that he made it on his own initiative with a bit of extra blackmail in mind. He also produced, under some pressure, three thousand quid in cash which he was paid by Foster. Where, I wonder, would Foster put his hands on that sort of money except from you? Anyway, this is what was recorded. Keith.'

Keith pressed the switch on the machine beside him. The reels began to turn in the recorder, and on the big monitor the interior of Chalet Sixteen appeared in full colour, as seen from above the fireplace.

'This is a copy,' Mrs Heller said. 'The original's at the bank.'

The tape had already been turned to the arrival of Foster. His image stood at the left of the picture, just inside the chalet door, a corpulent man but hard-looking. The shirt which hung open over his hairy body was marked with sweat. 'How you doing, friend of my youth?' His voice was rough and heavily accented with a near-Glasgow twang.

Close to the camera, only the top of Illingworth's head was visible, in poor focus. 'I'm about knackered,' he said thickly.

'But you enjoyed yourself?' Foster walked over to take the other chair. The picture was of an almost empty room, but the voices came over loudly and clearly. 'The girl was good?'

'The best. If there's any trick she didn't know, I don't know it either. I'm grateful for the introduction.'

'More than an introduction.'

'No.' From the movement of his head, Illingworth seemed to be struggling to get to his feet. He gave up the effort. 'I'll pay my whack,' he said. 'I don't accept that sort of hospitality.'

'Suit yourself, chiel. But Humbert Brown can afford it.'

'Who?' From a slurred croak Illingworth's voice rose to a squawk.

'Humbert Brown. I work for them now. Didn't you know? They want you to shut up about the Firth Bay job. You going to do that?'

'No way,' Illingworth said. 'I'm not changing. Anywhere I think there's been backhanders, I'll speak out. It's the on'y thing in the world I feel strongly about.'

'Is it by God?' Foster's voice became ominous. 'I wonder who'll listen to you when it's known you screwed your own sister.' When the other man remained silent, Foster spoke on, apparently answering some gesture or expression. 'Yes. Quite true. That hen's your long-lost baby sister.'

Illingworth dragged up a faint whisper. 'Not true.'

'Aye it is. And I've the whole thing on video-tape. I'll play it over to you if you want. It's good viewing. It'll go great on stag nights. And that's where it'll go if we have any more trouble from you. There's no mistaking your faces – it's good that you both faced the same way. You're ours now, chiel, and don't you forget it.'

Illingworth got to his feet with an effort. Expecting an attack, Foster got up quickly, but Illingworth made a rush for the bathroom door. The sound of vomiting came through, 'Aye,' said Foster. 'Just you have a chat wi' God on the big white phone. But he'll not help you now. Sorry, and all that, but I had too much to lose. I had my head in a sling with the firm, and this'll get me out. It was you or me, pal, and you got my vote.' He yawned and scratched himself. 'I'm going back to my chalet to flake out for a bit. Pick me up whenever you're fit to drive. No hurry. If she comes back again, well, it's paid for. No hard feelings, eh?'

He walked out, leaving the door ajar. Illingworth staggered out of the bathroom and looked around him. He seemed surprised to find the room empty. The colour recording showed the whiteness around his lips and ears, and the cold sweat on his forehead. He stood, swaying, in the centre of the floor. Keith thought that he had never seen a man so destroyed and yet still ready to fight. As the recording ended, he was staring to the side of the picture in the direction of the wall with the guns.

'Small wonder,' Debbie Heller said, 'that the poor sod lost his head and killed Foster.'

If Howarth was moved at all, it was not by compunction. There was a cold glitter in his eye. 'How did he kill him? Do you know?'

'We know. Mr Calder figured it out for us. But we're not saying. This is what they call a need-to-know operation.'

Howarth nodded towards Keith. 'He knows.'

'He already knew. And I needed a man with me.' She smiled

150

maliciously. 'I'm only a poor, weak woman.'

To Keith's surprise, Howarth smiled back. 'You're a poor, weak carton of dynamite,' he said. 'Well, how he did it is immaterial. The question is, can you prove it?'

'We could if we wanted to.'

'Let's get together on this,' Howarth said. He lit another cigarette. 'With the capital at your command, the facilities of this establishment, my organisation and now that tape to keep Illingworth out of our hair, we'd have a license to print money. We could get our hands into almost every speculative commercial development in the country.'

'It's an interesting proposition,' Mrs Heller said. (Keith felt the hairs prickle up the back of his neck.)

'You're on, then?'

'No, Mr Howarth, we're not on. I thought you'd have known by now that we don't play that sort of game. We sell bodies, but bodies that want to be sold. We deal squarely with everybody and give value for money. There's not many businesses can make that boast.'

'A high moral tone's all very well, but I never thought to hear a tart turn down a few million pounds.'

'An ex-tart. And you've heard it now.'

Howarth stubbed his cigarette out violently. He only wished that it could have been on one of the more sensitive parts of Mrs Heller's delicate body. 'You're in no position to refuse. All that my firm has at risk is that one of its members, now missing, tried a bit of blackmail on his own account. He may have got killed for it – I wouldn't know about that. And if he got killed he got killed for it here. And you know it. You've failed to report it to the police. Duty, I think, requires me to go to the police. So does elementary prudence. It's unfortunate that your best-heeled clients will shy away the minute you get involved in that kind of an investigation. I'm afraid you'll be ruined.'

Debbie Heller gave a small snort of laughter. 'There's no such thing as bad publicity,' she said.

'Full-page advertisements in Penthouse won't keep you laughing in the jail,' Howarth retorted. 'You've suppressed evidence, conspired to pervert the course of justice . . . I wouldn't want to be in your shoes after I've told my tale to the Regional Crime Squad. I know Superintendant Meikle well.'

'I dare say that I know him better,' Mrs Heller said, 'and I don't think my shoes would suit you at all. I've listened to your ultimatum, now you'd better hear mine.

'I told you that I'd stopped a few mouths. Now you'd better do the same, including your own and those two shamuses you hired. All they want is money. Provide it.

'Foster left a widow. See that she gets her pension. He was killed at work.

'If you agree to my conditions, I'll agree to you being allowed to tender, competitively, for the Firth Bay project. Oh yes, I know you've got three of the committee in your pocket with lucrative consultancies to your allied companies; but without my financing the project won't go ahead at all.'

Howarth's face was openly sneering. 'With tendering as fierce as it is just now, a winning tender won't show any profit worth a damn. Would ten grand to you personally change your attitude?'

'Only to the extent that if you dare suggest such a thing again I'll have you barred from tendering at all.' She paused and moistened her lips. A tiny flash of light pulsed at an ornament on her bracelet, from a tremor of tension that ran through her slight frame. Then it disappeared as she lifted her hand to see her watch. 'In a little over two hours, your men are due to arrive and pour concrete in the bottom of the new pool.'

'So?'

'Unfortunately for you, Mr Howarth, you can trust me but I'd be a fool to trust you. You said that I could shut mouths. I shut the mouth of my porter by making him lift a panel of reinforcement, dig a grave and carry the body down to it. He thought that he was doing it for money, but he was recorded on video-tape every inch of the way. Your man Foster taught us the trick and it's a good one. That should shut his mouth for keeps.

'Beside the grave are two bags of quicklime. My proposition, Mr Howarth, is that you go down to the bottom of the pool. You cover the body with lime, and then with clay Then you replace the reinforcement. You do all this before your men get here. If you don't –'

'I'll see you in hell first!'

Mrs Heller's hand went out to the console on her desk. 'Very possible,' she said. The door opened. Three porters came in, one of them incongruously wheeling a trolley of bottles. There were no glasses. The porters ranged themselves in a line, two boxers and a wrestler. They did not look formidable unless you knew their background. Howarth knew it, and he lost colour.

'If he interrupts me again,' Mrs Heller said, 'hit him. Don't knock him out and don't mark him, but hurt him.'

Howarth opened his mouth to protest, and shut it again. For the first time he lost his air of being in command of the discussion. He was used to power but not to violence. The volcano of his ulcer was spewing hot lava. He fumbled for a bismuth tablet.

Mrs Heller spoke again, and the undercurrent of Glasgow was stronger in her voice. 'If you don't do what I tell you,' she said, 'you'll be found in your car in a few hours time, drunk to the world. Your car will be damaged, and your boot will have sprung open in the accident. In it will be Foster's body. You can make what allegations you like. If they concern us, there will be no evidence whatever to support them. On the other hand, you will be amazed to find what evidence turns up against you. I'll not tell you what it'll be, because forewarned is forearmed; but a lot of thought went into it and, as you said, if I want my staff to jump through hoops, through hoops they jump.'

She looked up at her porters. She was still totally in command, but over her pretty face was a great sadness. She got to her feet as if she was tired to death. 'I don't even want to know his answer,' she said. 'I'll leave him to think it over. If he says yes, see that he gets on with it and then hold him incommunicado until the concreting's done. Mr Calder will make the recording. If he says no, let him choose his tipple, fill him full of it and then you know what to do.

'You see, Mr Howarth, I don't believe that you knew nothing of what Foster was going to do. Your agents were here too soon. And Foster had too easy access to too much money. And you heard him on the recording. It was as near as he could come to an apology. He didn't say "I've too much to gain"; he said "I've too much to lose". Those things between them drop you right in the clag, Mr Howarth.'

She walked out of the room.

Keith Calder came back slowly into the reality of the hotel room, and of Donald Illingworth sitting apathetically. The image of that scene in Debbie Heller's office overlaid it like a scene reflected in the glass over a painting. Even while he was remembering the tussle between the hard-headed businessman and the harder-headed ex-whore, something had been needling at the fringes of his consciousness. Something that he had seen or heard. Something in the recording. Something that he had noticed without noticing until his memory threw it up. Suddenly, it was clear in his mind.

'You stupid, quixotic, hare-brained cunt!' he said, and if the words were harsh there was more than a little admiration in his tone. 'You didn't shoot him at all.'

Illingworth sat up straight, and Keith recognised the nervous intensity which had been lacking before. 'I shot him,' he said. 'I've already admitted it.'

'Admitting is one thing, doing's another,' Keith said. 'I thought your manner didn't quite add up right. It was evasive without being guilty.'

Illingworth bunched his fists and started to get up, but Keith reached out and pushed him gently back into the chair. 'Damn you!' Illingworth said. 'I've admitted it. Can't you leave it alone? What business is it of yours?'

'You said you weren't a fighter. Don't make me prove it. Business? You made it the business of Personal Service when you buried a body on their land. They asked me to look into it for them. So that makes it my business.' Keith shook his head. 'You looked as guilty as hell. But still, I should have known better. A dozen wee contradictions have been niggling away at me, but I was so sure I knew it all that I ignored them or explained them away to myself. Just for starters, you're just the type to do every bit of it – except pull the trigger.' Keith stared into Illingworth's face, remembering other men whose cast of feature held the same racial and glandular imprints. One thing that he had learned in life was that if two men looked alike they reacted similarly. 'You could plan and reason and theorise about death, but you lack the kind of ruthlessness that could take the final step.'

Illingworth opened his mouth to protest and closed it without speaking. He shook his head, but mechanically and without any attempt to be convincing.

'Another thing that nagged at me,' Keith went on, 'was that Hilary took a hell of a time to fetch up at her next appointment. But I pushed it into the back of my mind, because I long since gave up wondering how a woman can take so long to do anything. Then again, I wondered how a client, and on his first visit, would know enough about the audiovisual system to be able to shoot a man without being rumbled by the porter on duty. But a girl with a husky voice, deliberately pitching it lower, could get away with it.

'I remember telling my wife that this wasn't a woman's act. But I hadn't bargained for your sister – a girl brought up in a house hung with old guns, so much a part of her childhood that it gave her a sense of homeliness to have the Millmont House collection hanging in her chalet. And I hadn't allowed for her having a brother to load it for her.

'Your story of going along to Chalet Fifteen and confronting Henry Foster is too convincing and circumstantial to be a lie. I think it was true as far as it went.

'But now, something else has come back to me. When I first went and looked at Hilary's chalet, Number Sixteen, I was taken with her cassette-radio on the bedside table. It's an expensive one, in an alligator case. Then, when I met your sister, I never saw her but she was lugging about an alligator-skin handbag of the same size and shape. At a guess, they were made and bought as a matching pair. I never looked inside it, but I suppose that, over and above the things women carry in handbags, the girls at Millmont House would have certain specialised items of ... toiletry.'

'You don't have to pussyfoot around the subject,' Illingworth said gruffly. 'I've faced up to it. They'd have pills or contraceptives, deodorants, lubricants, disinfectants and God knows what-all.'

'That's what I supposed,' Keith said. 'And all personal to the individual. But on the videotape of Foster giving you the blackmail treatment, it was the handbag on the bedside table, not the

155

radio. I remember seeing the clasp, without noticing it at the time. And she was away to keep another appointment. She must have picked up the wrong one. And she certainly wouldn't do business without its contents. So she ... came ... back! Tell me what happened,' Keith finished gently.

Illingworth started to shake his head again, but in mid-shake he sighed and then the dam burst. 'You know so much,' he said. 'You may as well know the rest ... off the record. I can always leave a note, giving my official version. Hilary came back for her bag. When she was approaching the place where you turn off for Chalet Fifteen she saw me going that way and carrying the pistol. Well, even a man would have been curious enough to follow. She heard the whole thing and when I went outside I found her waiting for me. You were right, when it came to the point I just didn't have the guts to pull the trigger. Behind me, Foster was laughing his head off, I could still hear him.

'It must have been a hell of a shock for her, finding out like that that I was her brother. I was shattered. I could have collapsed on the spot. My brain seemed to have ground to a halt, and I was thinking through a layer of cotton wool. But she was absolutely calm. She didn't say a word, just took the pistol out of my hand and walked in through the door. I heard Foster start to say something. There was a shot and I heard a voice speaking to the porter. It was more like a man's voice, and for a moment I thought that *he'd* shot *her*. Then she came out and handed me the videotape. She led, almost carried, me back to Number Sixteen and she spelled out exactly what we were going to do. She's all there is Hilary – even as a child she could stay calm and use her loaf when I was all of a dither. She stayed with me until she was sure that I'd got it. Then she gave me a quick kiss, a sisterly one, and went off to her next appointment.'

They fell silent. Keith thought of the girl, brave and decisive. He wondered whether her motives had been selfish or noble. She sounded like a useful girl to have around in time of crisis. He wondered how Molly would have reacted to similar circumstances.

While these speculations were flickering over the surface of his mind, at a deeper level he was sifting and sorting the known facts.

156

The new story, as told by Illingworth, hung together; but if it ironed out a few blemishes in the story it introduced some fresh ones. He wondered whether this was the truth at last. Well, while Illingworth was talking it might be the time to find out. 'Why were you carrying all your gear in the car,' he asked, 'almost a week before the Game Fair?'

Illingworth looked at him vaguely and made a visible effort to think back to less haunted days. 'It seems so long ago,' he said. 'I was heading for Newcastle to inspect some site-works. I've a pal lives near Catterick, an old class-mate; sometimes we shoot targets together. But with this on my mind I decided I couldn't face it. He wasn't expecting me.'

'And that's why you had a ball with you, of course. Why did Foster come in your car?'

'He seemed to think that I might cry off unless he stayed close and egged me on. He said he might visit the Newcastle office of his firm and go back on the train.' Illingworth sighed, shudderingly. 'Do you have to ask all these bloody questions?'

'Just tying up loose ends.' Keith scoured his mind for more questions, to keep Illingworth's thoughts on hard facts and away from dangerous abstractions.'Your sister could have made investigation much more difficult if she'd delayed finding the bullet-hole for a few months. Why didn't she? That was one of the things that steered me away from her.'

'And that was why, partly,' Illingworth said. 'I was beyond any chance of straight thinking, but I remember what Hilary said. She thought that it was a toss-up whether she gave herself the best image by finding the chair quickly or to wait a while. She'd decided to wait. We swapped the chairs over so that she could have the bloodstained one, complete with bullet-hole, under her hand. That way, she could make the discovery in her own good time.'

'But she didn't.'

'No. As I told you, my mind was ... clouded. She helped me carry the chairs, because I was as weak as a baby and those chairs weigh a ton. In swapping them over, we'd left her chalet short of a chair-back. She went back to Number Fifteen to pinch one, but

I'd pulled the door shut. An extra visit would have been recorded and might have been noticed later. We looked round some other chalets, but they were either locked or occupied. So we let it go. She said she'd use the missing chair-back as a reason for finding the hole and the stains. And one other thing she said. She said . . . that . . . if there was any question of my being blamed, she'd confess and take the rap.' He blew his nose wetly, and surreptitiously wiped his eyes.

Keith had run out of questions. 'But,' he said, 'you decided to go one better. You were going to top yourself and leave a note taking all the blame?'

Illingworth nodded. 'I still am,' he said. He got slowly to his feet and took the four paces to the open window.

Keith stayed seated. A wrestling-match would not solve anything. His back felt cold. 'No you're bloody well not,' he said.

'You can't stop me.' Illingworth sat down on the sill of the open window and rocked gently to and fro. Each time he leaned back, his heels lifted off the carpet. He was eight floors above a paved terrace.

'I could stop you,' Keith said. 'But there'd be no point. You could do it as soon as my back was turned.'

'Right.' Illingworth swayed back and nearly went for the long dive. Only an involuntary kick of his legs brought him back in balance.

'I can only point out that if you kill yourself you'll drop everybody in the shit head-first. And that includes your sister. Christ, we've all been covering up for you, suppressing evidence, burying bodies and committing blackmail, and if there's any real investigation we're done for.'

'Hilary will be all right.'

'Wishful thinking,' Keith said. He could see Illingworth nerving himself for the last lean back. He sought frantically for more argument and, to his own surprise, found it. 'It doesn't matter how many notes you've left. If there's an investigation, Hilary goes up the river unless you're there to take the blame off her. And, don't forget, you're the one that was being blackmailed, not your sister. A court would go easier on you.

'As things stand at the moment, it's a billion to one against any

158

investigation because we've stopped every hole. But if you're stupid enough to take the quick way down to street level, and if you've left a note, and if I can't find it and tear it up, then there's going to be an investigation right enough. In among many, many other things, the fuzz are going to want to know why a big wheel in Humbert Brown told them that Foster had gone abroad. His only loophole would be to prove that he was being blackmailed by Mrs Heller. Next thing, the cops have most of the story and she has to give up the videotape of the scene between you and Foster. How long do you think it would take a trained detective to spot that handbag?'

Illingworth made a sudden grab at the window-frame. He leaned forward into the room. 'You could go back and destroy that tape,' he said.

'If you're prepared to drop the rest of us in it,' Keith said, 'why the hell should any of us add to our crimes to protect your sister? No, if you jump our only course of action is to run screaming to the police, shouting "Look what we've just found", and give them *everything.*'

Illingworth stood up. He walked on quaking knees to where Keith sat, and stood irresolute.

'Don't try to jump me,' Keith said, 'or I'll break both your arms. You said yourself that you're no kind of a fighter. Your only way to protect Hilary is to come back and take up your life again. Then, if questions are ever raised, you can do your shining-armour bit. But it won't come to that. Never.'

There was another silence, longer than ever before. Illingworth collapsed back into his chair. Keith took one look at his face, got up in his turn and walked to the window. A tourist ship was coming to anchor in the bay. Behind him, he heard the first sob. He wanted to go and comfort the weeping man in his arms but his upbringing was against it. He stood where he was, sympathetic but acutely embarrassed. Even when the sobbing ceased, he stood where he was. But he kept a firm grip on the window-frame. After all, he was so far the only person to guess the truth.

159

Fifteen

Chief Inspector Munro lounged at ease in the uncomfortable chair in his uncomfortable room in the very uncomfortable building which still, although in its hundredth year, served the Lothian and Borders Constabulary as its Newton Lauder Headquarters. Before Munro's desk stood Sergeant Ritchie, and his discomfort outdid all the rest. For most of an hour Munro had been roasting him for his alleged favours to Keith Calder. Ritchie's back was sore and his feet hurt, but his dignity hurt worst of all. Munro's Hebridean tongue could flay like a razor. And Ritchie could not take comfort in his own innocence, for he was guilty and he knew it.

Munro relished the English language for its wealth of epithets – so lacking in his native Gaelic – but even the longest-winded chief inspector must eventually exhaust them. 'I do not suppose that you have made any progress in the matter of the two men hung on the tree?'

'No, sir.'

'With Calder involved, I hardly expected any,' Munro said, 'so I have been researching the matter, by telephone, on my own account. We will just run over the facts.' (Ritchie groaned softly and shifted from one foot to the other.) 'The man in hospital, Bardolph, is one of those private investigators. You may well think,' Munro said with grim humour, 'that he deserved what he got, but even a ... real-life private eye is entitled to the protection of the law, and he has it whether he wants it or not. He works usually with another man, Warrender, who answers the description of the other man at the tree. The agency for which they usually worked says that they are now freelance. The witness who released them was drawn to the place by the sound of a shot. There were pellets of shot in the sole of Bardolph's shoe. The shotgun is Calder's weapon.'

'With respect,' Ritchie broke in, 'it's his job and his hobby, no more than that.'

'Whenever Calder makes an enemy, which is too often for my liking, we find to our great surprise that he is carrying around a shotgun – and a perfectly valid written permission from a landowner to shoot the land. And I have seen him kill a man.'

'On your orders, sir, and to save your life.'

'That may be so, but it has no bearing. Next, a lorry-driver who passed that way saw Calder's car – very well,' Munro said irritably, 'a car the make and colour of Calder's – by the roadside. A grey Citroen stood nearby with its bonnet raised. The other witness, the farm-hand, thinks that it was Calder who drove away. It is a great pity that neither of them noted the numbers of the cars. The Vehicle Registration Centre in Swansea tells me that Warrender owns a grey Citroen. Bardolph is in hospital and – mark you this, Ritchie – Warrender has not been seen again since he was let down from the tree. On a circumstantial level, the cars and the shot connect Calder with the two men.'

'Circumstantial,' Ritchie said, 'and very speculative.'

'I am aware of it. Now, going back in time but forward in logic, a grey Citroen was seen in the lay-by overlooking Millmont House on several occasions over a two-day period immediately prior to these events. That provides a loose but possible connection, through the two men, between Calder and,' Munro flushed darkly, 'that abominable establishment. Moving forward again in time, Calder vanished overnight, ostensibly to Dundee, and reappeared with his face injured. Mrs James, with whom he has long been as thick as any number of thieves, told us a cock-and-bull story about her husband being missing. We held Calder for three days, but we did not look for Mr James, only for his body. Mr James then reappeared, refusing to give any explanation as to where he had been.

'Not even yourself, Ritchie, would suggest that that story was anything but a fabrication, although we can not prove that Mrs James was not honestly mistaken. It was intended to distract us. But to distract us from what? It had us looking in Dundee. Where should we have been looking, Ritchie?'

Ritchie sighed. He was sick of Munro and his damned, pedantic Highland drawl. 'I don't know, sir,' he said.

'Then I will see whether we can't reason it out. We will ask

161

ourselves a few questions and see what answers we get. How did Calder's face get marked?'

'In the fight with the two men,' Ritchie suggested.

'The witness who saw him drive away said that he seemed unmarked. And such bruising as Calder suffered would soon have made it impossible for him to drive. So he must have been in another fight. The man Warrender drove off as soon as he was released from the tree, leaving others to attend to Bardolph and get him to hospital. Where was he going?'

Ritchie shrugged his tired shoulders.

'In pursuit of Calder, of course,' Munro said. 'Calder had hitched them to the tree to prevent such pursuit, but he had not bargained on the sound of the shot attracting help to them so soon. And where was Calder going? That place is not on the shortest route between Newton Lauder and Millmont House, but nor would it be an unreasonable route. I think that Calder was going to that house of shame. And now, why has neither hide nor hair been seen of the man Warrender since then?'

Ritchie came out in a cold sweat. He knew Keith Calder more intimately than Munro could ever do; and Munro's insinuations were by no means beyond the bounds of credibility. 'He could be in a different hospital under an assumed name,' the sergeant suggested. 'Or he could be in hiding, for fear of – er – Mr Calder.'

'Or ... he ... could ... be ... dead,' Munro said, stabbing at Ritchie with a bony finger to emphasise his words. 'I think that he caught up with Calder, and there was another fight, and Calder killed him. And then why was such an elaborate red herring drawn across the trail? There was no apparent connection between Warrender and Calder, or not so far as we know. If Calder killed the man, he might well have left him lying. If it was self-defence, he might even have come to us himself. But there was a connection, probably a disreputable connection, between the man Warrender and Millmont House. I think that Warrender caught up with Calder there, and was killed in a second fight. But that establishment could never stand up to the scandal of a body, dead of foul play; and they have the money with which to bend others to their convenience. The red herring was dragged so that we would be holding Calder here and looking for his partner in the

162

Tay, while all the time Mr James was driving Warrender's body to some other part of the country and disposing of it.'

'Wallace James is not a man I could see doing such a thing,' Ritchie said.

'It had to be James. Calder's face was marked, so he had to be the stalking-horse.'

Ritchie was becoming increasingly unhappy. Munro's long-standing belief that Keith Calder would balk at nothing was leading the inspector to formulate theories to which no other officer would be likely to give credence – except Ritchie himself. 'This is a matter for the C.I.D.,' he said, 'not for us uniformed lads.'

Munro slumped back in his chair and scratched the back of his neck. 'That is just the very devil of it,' he said. 'C.I.D. have had enough information out of that place over the years to fill a Bible – or a jail. They will want hard evidence before they make any move that will lose them that friendship.'

'We do not have any,' Ritchie said firmly. He looked over Munro's shoulder and out of the window. Surely he would soon be able to escape for a good sit-down ...

'Not so hasty,' Munro said. 'I will tell you what I have been doing while you were sitting on your backside. It is a pity that people do not carry number-plates like cars,' he said severely, as if that omission were all the sergeant's fault. 'It would make our work that much easier. But these businessmen go everywhere by car, and cars carry number-plates. The man on the beat never recognises a man from his description, but even you, Ritchie, can read a number-plate. So I asked Swansea for the numbers of the cars of every person I could think of as possibly being involved with this case. And I asked all forces to keep an eye out for them.'

'Very interesting,' said Ritchie.

'It is,' Munro said. 'It can be very interesting, what one can learn through car numbers. When Mr James came back to Newton Lauder he came back in an Edinburgh taxi,' despite himself, Munro sounded impressed by such extravagance, 'and unlike our various witnesses I had the sense to write down the number. Edinburgh police have spoken with the driver. He picked up Mr James in Waverley Station, and thought it almost certain that he had come off the train from Dundee, which started from Aberdeen. Now why, we wonder, was Mr James travelling by train?'

'He's missing three fingers,' Ritchie said. 'He might well prefer to do a long journey that way.'

When Munro grinned his bony face became a skull, fleshless. Ritchie averted his eyes. 'There could be other reasons,' Munro said. 'The Aberdeen police report that Warrender's car, the grey Citroen, is abandoned near the docks up there.'

'Abandoned, sir? Or parked?'

'Parked, Ritchie, would suggest that somebody was likely to come back for it. I had them tow it to the police garage and force the boot. No body in it,' Munro said with regret, 'but their forensic laddies are giving it the going-over and we shall see what we shall see. Do you know what we will find, Ritchie?'

'Aye,' Ritchie said. 'I ken what you expect to find.' He shifted from one foot to the other again and eased his aching back.

'Calder killed Warrender at Millmont House. I don't know why, not yet, but there are enough women there for them to fight over, and I have been prophesying for years that one day Calder would kill a man over a woman. Perhaps Warrender was trying blackmail – he has that reputation. But, whyever, the deed was done. Now, Mrs Heller would not be standing for bodies at Millmont House at all. Calder went away. Mrs James reported her husband missing, believed murdered by Calder, while Mr James drove Warrender's car, with its owner's body in the boot, up to Aberdeen and came back by train.'

'And took four days over it.'

'From that,' Munro said, 'we may gain a clue as to how the body was disposed of. Aberdeen City Police are looking into that end of it. And when I get evidence from Aberdeen ... well, Calder may have fled the country, but C.I.D. will have to take action and they can squeeze Mr and Mrs James and that Heller woman until – what is the expression? – until the pips squeak.'

'The Calders went to Madeira on holiday.'

'A very sudden holiday.' Munro paused and a bleak smile spread over his face. 'I will tell you a funny thing, Ritchie. I knew all along that there had been a killing. I thought that it was the man Foster whose wife reported him missing. But that report was withdrawn. I spoke to the man's employers, one of the biggest firms of contractors in the country. I spoke to the deputy managing director himself. It seems that the man had gone abroad on the firm's business, and having had a tiff with his wife he did not bother to let her know.'

'Very funny,' Ritchie agreed stolidly.

'I have not come to the funny bit yet. It is that, because of my enquiries, I was able to help. Foster went abroad without saying where he had left the Jaguar car that he has from the firm. I was able to tell him that the car was parked at Inchgavie. He was very grateful. I think that we may have made a useful friend in that quarter.'

Ritchie sighed. He was coasting towards his pension and rarely volunteered for anything that could possibly be delegated to a subordinate. But well-developed instinct told him that he had better start being helpful or he would be on his feet until that pension matured. What was more, a similar instinct suggested that if Munro pursued his present lines of enquiry he might come up with something ... not a murder, perhaps, but something discreditable to Keith Calder. But Munro himself had just suggested a possible red herring.

'Inchgavie?' Ritchie said thoughtfully. 'Maybe the man was lifted from there by his murderer. Shall I just find out who lives nearby and see whether there is any one of them who might have a connection?'

Chief Inspector Munro turned the question over in his devious, Highland mind, quite unaware of how much might hang in the balance. Then, regretfully, he shook his head. 'No need for that,' he said. 'If the man's employer says that he is alive and abroad, then that is an end to it. The firm is building some houses nearby. No doubt he left the car there for safe-keeping and got one of the site staff to drive him to Dundee Airport or –'

The telephone made a noise which could stop even a chief inspector in full flood of speculation. 'Answer it,' Munro said.

Tiredly, Ritchie picked up the phone, but as he listened his tiredness fell away and there was a new glint in his eye. 'The Aberdeen City Police are on the line,' he told Munro. 'Mr Warrender has just stepped off the *St Clair* from Lerwick. He's in a terrible taking, they say, about his car being towed away and forced open. Would you speak to them?'

Chief Inspector Munro said that he would rather not.

Sixteen

Keith and Molly sat over the remains of breakfast on their balcony. Below them, the hotel swimming pool had been taken over by four of the local black swans, but a blonde in a bikini was swimming nervously in the furthest corner of the pool. She had been making eyes at Keith in the bar the night before.

'But I don't want to go home yet,' Molly said.

'I've done what I came for.'

'Well, I haven't. I came out for a holiday. It's been lovely swimming and sunbathing and having drinks by the pool, but I haven't been out of the hotel grounds. I want to see the Crater Village, and have rides in bullock-carts and wicker sledges and things. And there's plenty to interest you.' Keith looked down at the pool. Molly tossed down a well-aimed crust. The black swans made a rush, necks outstretched. The blonde screamed and fled from the pool. 'I didn't mean that,' Molly said with satisfaction. 'Vineyards and so on.'

'The grouse season starts soon,' Keith said.

'Not for ages.'

'But there's always a rush of guns for overhaul before then. And we've got tickets for the Billy Connolly concert.'

'Never mind the concert,' Molly said. She felt guilty. If Keith knew that she had given his precious tickets to the man who had threatened his family, he would be furious. Worse, he might be responsive to more trustworthy female company. 'If it's Deborah you're worried about,' she said, 'she'll be all right with Janet. And if Janet wants to get away, Mrs Heller said that she'd take Deborah for a few days.'

The idea of his infant daughter spending even a minute at Millmont House scandalised Keith. 'Certainly not,' he said. 'Under no circumstances does she go to Debbie Heller!'

'*Debbie* Heller?' Molly said sharply. 'Is that her name? Keith, when you insisted that we call our daughter Deborah –?'

'Good God, no! I only met her for the first time when this blew up. Ask Wallace.'

'Then why don't you want her to look after Deborah?'

'She's the wrong sort of person.' By now, Keith realised that he had put his foot firmly into it. He wondered whether to get Molly's mind off Mrs Heller by provoking some quite different quarrel, but decided against it. He would placate Molly, he decided, but not to the extent of staying on much longer in Madeira while the grouse season loomed ever nearer. 'She's a busy woman with no experience of babies,' he said. 'And I don't like being under an obligation to a client.'

'I see.' Molly wondered whether to work up a quarrel over Mrs Heller, to put Keith in the wrong and keep his mind off returning home too quickly. But she decided against it. Charity, after all, can cover up a multitude of sins. 'Perhaps you're right,' she said. 'Your sister might be better. We'll telephone later. Just for now, this sun's getting a bit hot. Why don't we think it over inside?'

Inside was a small room with a large, soft bed.

'Good idea,' Keith said. 'I'm glad you thought of that.'

Each breathed a sigh of relief. Their sins had not found them out.